"What are you doing here?" Ethan asked.

The familiar male voice swept straight through her, mocking any attempt to keep her emotions in check. Joanna stopped in her tracks. Stared.

The man, easily six foot four, froze in the open doorway. His eyes narrowed as they locked on to hers. The wind glued his brown suit jacket to his broad shoulders. The rain made his military-short hair glisten like polished onyx.

"Joanna?" The timbre of his voice darkened. The deep pitch of it filled up his chest and rumbled out in a seductive whisper.

"Ethan." Here. In the flesh. Impossibly bigger, broader, harder than the man she remembered. The silent intensity of his dark, nearly black eyes hit her like a sucker punch to the heart.

Ethan Bia.

The man she'd given her virginity and her young girl's heart to.

The man who'd taught her how to survive the mountains—and her family.

The man she'd walked away from fifteen years ago without ever looking back.

JULIE MILLER

PULLING *the* TRIGGER

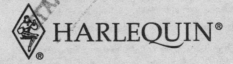

HARLEQUIN®

TORONTO • NEW YORK • LONDON
AMSTERDAM • PARIS • SYDNEY • HAMBURG
STOCKHOLM • ATHENS • TOKYO • MILAN • MADRID
PRAGUE • WARSAW • BUDAPEST • AUCKLAND

For my dad. Ace navigator extraordinaire. The most knowledgeable man I know when it comes to learning about a place and finding my way. Yep, there's double entendre there.

While Sleeping Ute Mountain and the Four Corners area of southwestern Colorado are real, full of stark beauty and dramatic landscapes, I've taken the liberty of creating some fictional places to serve the needs of the story. So if you do visit the area—and if you're a fan of history or geography I strongly encourage you to do so—you might not find all of the locations Ethan and Joanna visit on the map. But you will find friendly people and a beautiful part of the country.

ISBN-13: 978-0-373-69405-1

PULLING THE TRIGGER

Copyright © 2009 by Harlequin Books S.A.

Special thanks and acknowledgment to Julie Miller for her contribution to the Kenner County Crime Unit miniseries.

Recycling programs for this product may not exist in your area.

www.eHarlequin.com

Printed in U.S.A.

ABOUT THE AUTHOR

Julie Miller attributes her passion for writing romance to all those fairy tales she read growing up, and to shyness. Encouragement from her family to write down all those feelings she couldn't express became a love for the written word. She gets continued support from her fellow members of the Prairieland Romance Writers, where she serves as the resident "grammar goddess." This award-winning author and teacher has published several paranormal romances. Inspired by the likes of Agatha Christie and Encyclopedia Brown, Ms. Miller believes the only thing better than a good mystery is a good romance.

Born and raised in Missouri, she now lives in Nebraska with her husband, son and smiling guard dog, Maxie. Write to Julie at P.O. Box 5162, Grand Island, NE 68802-5162.

Books by Julie Miller

*The Precinct
**The Precinct: Vice Squad
†The Precinct: Brotherhood of the Badge

CAST OF CHARACTERS

Ethan Bia—Tied to Mother Earth in ways that sometimes defy science, this Native American tracker and former U.S. Army Ranger can find anyone, anywhere. He's trained to survive anything—except working with the woman he once loved again.

Joanna Rhodes—FBI Agent and interrogation specialist. When she left the reservation, her life was in a shambles. Now she's back home on an assignment that can make her career and break the case of a murdered fellow agent wide open. But a new name, a gun and a badge can't protect her vulnerable heart—or stop the nightmares of her past from trying to destroy her again.

Sherman Watts—The reservation's local drunk, or a link to the mob? This old friend from Joanna's past seems to have nine lives. And if nine aren't enough to survive, he'll take a few more.

Elizabeth Reddawn—Receptionist at the Kenner County Crime Unit. She knows the reservation's secrets.

Elmer Watts—Retired sheriff. A senile old man who remembers what he wants to.

Bart Flemming—KCCU's resident techno-wizard.

Ben Parrish—Is the FBI agent dead? Or has he betrayed them all?

Boyd Perkins—Hit man for the mob. Supposedly in Mexico.

Julie Grainger—Murdered FBI Agent.

Prologue

"I need you to disappear."

Sherman Watts drained the amber fire of whiskey from his shot glass and licked the dribble from his lips before putting the phone back to his ear and responding to his anonymous contact's hushed command. "What about my money?"

"You've gone through last month's payment already?"

It wasn't this loser's business how he spent his money or how fast he spent it. He'd earned a lot more than this secure cell phone he'd been given so their calls about confidential business couldn't be traced. "I was promised fifty thousand. Your people are ten grand short."

"I can deposit the installment into your account on Monday—under the guise of another government settlement payment. You know I can't authorize the payment any earlier than that. If I pay out the money too fast, it'll throw up a red flag, and someone might start nosing around in our business."

Someone else, you mean. Since the Kenner County Crime Unit and a cadre of FBI agents had come to Kenner City, Colorado, and the nearby Ute reservation where Sherman lived, investigating the murder of a lady agent who'd been messing with some people she ought not to have been messing with, there had been plenty of people nosing around. Funny how the man on the phone wasn't afraid of the hit man Sherman had been hiding on the rez and doing some odd jobs for. Funnier still how the man trying to give him orders could deal with two feuding Las Vegas crime families and keep a cool head, but he had a burr up his butt over the possibility of some accountant questioning why Sherman Watts finally had the money to buy a good bottle of whiskey instead of drinking the rotgut that had curdled his conscience years ago.

Sherman poured himself a second glass to wash down the bologna sandwich he'd eaten for lunch. "I'm perfectly comfortable here in Mesa Ridge." He took a sip and savored the smooth burn down his throat. "Besides, I thought it was my job to be the front man. Nobody knows the rez like I do. I can wander around any corner of it, talk to any man about anything and nobody blinks twice. I run Boyd Perkins's errands and get the information he needs so he can continue his search for that fifty million dollars from the Del Gardo family and take care of whatever private business he needs to. Hell, I'm doing such a good job that I hear the cops think Perkins is down in Mexico." Sherman plunked the glass down on the table in his trailer and sat up straight. Had something happened? This idiot might not be afraid of Boyd Perkins, but *he* was smart enough to know that crossing the ice-cold killer was a damn fool thing to do. He'd seen what Perkins was capable of when he'd disposed of that woman's body for him.

Screwing up and getting on the killer's bad side was not an option. "They think Perkins has left the country, right?"

"They have no clue he's still around."

"So what's the problem? Why do I need to skip town? And why isn't this coming from Perkins himself?"

"I'm doing you a favor, you coot. Giving you a heads-up."

He could tell from the condescending sneer in the man's tone that this wasn't about doing anybody a favor.

This guy was worried about covering his own backside.

"The FBI thinks you're involved in Julie Grainger's murder."

"The feds do?" Accomplice after the fact was definitely involved. He was screwed. Sherman pushed to his feet, stumbling over his chair as he went to the back of his trailer to grab a bag and start packing.

"The feds, the crime unit—they're all one team now. And they think you may know something. They're bringing in some hotshot profiler from D.C. to question you."

"What?"

"One of their own agents is dead. They may not have evidence to charge you with anything, but they're going to explore every possible lead on the case. And right now, that's you."

Screw that. He pulled his gun from his top dresser drawer and tucked it into the back of his jeans. Two boxes of bullets landed in the bottom of his pack. "Who else are they questioning?"

"No one. Like I said, they don't know that Perkins is

still in the neighborhood. But with the way you get around to every bar, whorehouse and the casino, I'm sure they want to ask if you've seen anyone matching his description."

Sherman dropped his bag back onto the bed. These past six months working for the Nicky Wayne crime family out of Vegas had given him the best money ticket of his life. He wasn't going to give it up if the feds just wanted to show him some pictures and ask if he knew a guy. "I can always say no. They've got nothing they can hold me on. You're just worried that I'll mention these phone calls, and then they'll figure out they have a traitor in their midst."

The lengthy pause indicated that Sherman had struck a nerve. "You've got nothing on me. No name. No ID. But can you still say no when the detox kicks in? Can you keep your mouth shut about Perkins? About Grainger's murder? Do you really want to take the fall for our crimes? This is a federal investigator they're bringing in, Watts, not some good ol' boy sheriff who'll give you a sip from his own flask and let you walk away. I hear she's tough. She'll break you."

"She?" He took the news like a punch to the gut.

Hell. It was a woman who had turned him to drink in the first place. Some woman or other always seemed to be standing in the way of what he deserved. His high school sweetheart, Naomi, had married his best friend, Ralph Kuchu, instead of him. Eighteen years later, Naomi had been drunk enough to get herself and Ralph both killed in a car wreck—taking the woman Sherman loved and the money Ralph owed him to their graves.

Women were good for one thing. Sobering him up and poking questions at him wasn't it.

And if she did flash her boobs or nag him enough and get him to reveal what he knew about Julie Grainger's murder or Boyd Perkins's whereabouts, then he'd be a dead man. He was only useful to Perkins and the family he worked for as long as he kept his mouth shut.

"All right. I can hide out for a few days." Sherman carried his bag out to the table and packed the whiskey bottle in with a change of socks and some fishing gear. He grabbed his sleeping bag from the closet and tied it to his pack. "Let Perkins and Mr. Wayne know that I'm out of here."

After disconnecting the call, Sherman opened the trailer door and studied the sky. Clouds were gathering with the promise of spring rain in the next twenty-four hours, give or take. That was good. It'd be hell to sleep in, as the temperature in the mountains was still cold on June nights. But rain also meant he wouldn't leave any tracks. He reached for his black, flat-brimmed hat and pulled it on over scraggly hair that was still as black as it had been the day he was born over fifty years ago. With his survival skills, he could last for weeks up in the red rocks and cliffs of the Mesa Verde range.

He could last as long as he had something to drink.

And no woman got in his way.

Chapter One

Special Agent Joanna Rhodes stepped off the puddle jumper flight from Durango into the rain at Kenner City, Colorado.

Though the other two passengers on the same plane made a dash for the shelter of the terminal, Joanna stood on the tarmac, surveying the stark, dramatic landscape of red rock mountains and barren desert spaces of the Four Corners region of the state. Awe-inspiring. Rich in history and mystique. Majestic. She'd read all the descriptors in tourism magazines and advertisements for the nearby casino.

But she couldn't see the beauty. She could barely feel the cool drizzle of rain spitting against her face. An oppressive sense of the world closing in around her, so at odds with the rugged, wide-open spaces, made it difficult to catch her breath.

"Suck it up, girl," Joanna whispered between clenched teeth, her nostrils flaring as she pulled her shoulders back and ordered her lungs to expand. It wasn't the altitude or the faint chill of early spring in the air that had grabbed hold of her. It wasn't the rain, kicking up a familiar, omnipresent dust and washing the scent of ozone down to her level, that made moving from this spot so difficult. It was the memories swirling inside her head, attacking her from every direction, that made this homecoming feel like a walk down a long corridor at a maximum-security prison, ending at a windowless cell with her name on it.

"That's the power of positive thinking," she chided herself with sarcasm, hating that her thoughts had gone off on the morbid metaphor. Fanciful images of any kind didn't fit with the practical, efficient persona she'd worked so hard to cultivate. This wasn't supposed to be a stroll down memory lane for her. "Focus on the work."

She was here to break open a case that the bureau, local law enforcement and the Kenner County Crime Lab had been investigating for five months now. Solve the murder of a federal agent in the area and uncover suspected links to the feuding Wayne and Del Gardo crime families out of Las Vegas. Find a lead on the missing fifty million dollars that the late crime boss, Vincent Del Gardo, had allegedly hid in the Four Corners area.

All she had to do was face down a nightmare from her past to get the answers they needed.

No small task on any front.

This was her assignment. She'd been personally requested by the Durango bureau office because of her ethnic background and ties to the area. Her boss in D.C. had assured her it was a career-making opportunity she'd be foolish to pass up. Besides, a job was a job. And she was damn good at hers.

Blinking the moisture from her long dark eyelashes,

Joanna checked the Glock 9 mm in the holster on her belt, as well as the FBI shield clipped beside it. Then she rebuttoned her pin-striped blazer and shook her ponytail down the center of her back.

"Piece of cake." Armed inside and out, she pulled up the handle on her overnight suitcase and strode toward the terminal.

"Agent Rhodes?" The glass double doors swung open and a tall, lanky man wearing a tuxedo with a cowboy hat and boots jogged out to meet her.

Instinctively, she halted and retreated half a step, her hand hovering near her gun, waiting for the man to identify himself.

"Didn't see you inside and thought I'd missed you. Sorry I'm running late. I had to pick up my wife and son and give away a bride before I could get here." He stopped a few feet away and tipped the brim of his hat before extending his hand in greeting. "I'm Patrick Martinez."

"Joanna Rhodes." Recognizing the name and the general description of dark hair and Irish-blue eyes given her by the bureau chief in Durango, Jerry Ortiz, she reached out to shake hands with the Kenner County sheriff. "You're not late, Sheriff. But I'd like to remind you that I could just as easily have rented a car and driven myself to your office."

He grinned. "Well, that wouldn't say very much for western hospitality, now, would it."

Knowing she was meant to smile at the friendly remark, she curved her mouth into a practiced arc. But when he reached for the handle of her suitcase, Joanna tightened her grip. Long before she'd reached the age of thirty-three, she'd learned to take care of herself in every way that mattered. "I've got it."

With a nod, he turned to walk beside her. "Then let's get you out of the rain and get you briefed on the investigation." Despite her show of independence, his longer stride got him to the doors first, and he pulled one open for her. He glanced up at the late afternoon's overcast sky as she walked through. "We're expecting storms on and off all weekend long. This little sprinkle is just the prelude."

She remembered the all or nothing weather patterns from her childhood. Summers could be beastly hot and dry, yet still be chilly at night. Winters were frigid, especially up in the mountains. And the transitional seasons in between promised torrential rains and flash floods, or blizzards, depending on the temperature. The area was probably going through its spring thaw right now, when massive snowmelts at the higher elevations filled the rivers and streams in the area—the same streambeds that would be bone dry come autumn. But she wasn't here to reminisce or discuss the weather. "How far are we from your office? I understand it shares a building with the crime unit?"

Once they cleared the terminal, the sheriff pointed to the officially marked black Suburban parked at the curb. With a beep from his key chain, he opened the back door behind the passenger seat. "You can toss your bag in here."

"Thank you."

His cowboy-style manners were charming but unnecessary. And once they were both inside the car, he seemed to accept that she was more interested in answers than in making new friends. "We've got a smoothly integrated system here in Kenner County. Budget constraints being what they are, the practicality of housing the area law enforcement units in one location made it a no-brainer. A briefing room, locker rooms, executive offices, plus the interview rooms, lineup room and temporary lockup are located on the first two floors, while most of the crime lab is housed upstairs on the third. We've got a fourth floor for storage." He shifted into Drive and pulled onto the highway leading into town. "We'll be there in ten minutes."

Through the rhythmic swish of the windshield wipers, Joanna watched the landscape change from scrub brush to the metal prefab buildings of a growing industrial park. They passed a neat and tidy residential area nestled in the foothills, filled with square, pueblo-style houses, bungalows and larger Victorian reproduction homes. Finally, Sheriff Martinez turned his car toward the brick and stone buildings that marked the downtown area. Kenner City was a quaint, bustling enterprise of a town, nestled in a bowl between mountain peaks. It boasted striped awnings and pinewood balconies, and flags flew above nearly every storefront and business.

Not one trailer park in sight. No run-down liquor store on the main drag. No tattered teenage girl running the streets, looking for her parents in seedy bars and back alleys, hoping they'd be happy drunk and cooperate with her efforts to get them safely home, instead of mean drunk and belligerent, or just flat passed out from whatever party or paycheck they'd drunk their way through on any given night.

Everything here was charming and well kept and scrupulously clean—a far cry from the Ute reservation where she'd grown up, just a few more miles down the road.

She knew she was expected to say something, to make conversation to pass the drive time. But Joanna had made a career out of watching and assessing before she spoke, learning to listen without saying more than was required. Even before her training, idle chitchat had never come easily for her.

The sheriff didn't seem to have that problem, however. "The hotel where you're booked is just a block from our location, and I figured you'd be doing your interview of the suspect there. If you do want to go somewhere, one of my deputies will be available to drive you. Or we can loan you a vehicle if it's not in use." He slowed as they drove through the heart of downtown, touching his hat to pedestrians hurrying along the wide sidewalks. As they passed the last few businesses, he pointed out a diner-style restaurant with bright lights and lots of windows called the Morning Ray Café. "That's my mom's place. You can get all three meals there. It's good, down-home cookin' that'll fill you up."

The gleam of pride was obvious in his tone and smile. Joanna's mother's idea of a home-cooked meal had involved ripping open packages and zapping them in the microwave—when she remembered to fix any meal at all for her daughter. Joanna had turned herself into a fairly accomplished cook by the time she'd finished the third grade, simply as a matter of survival. But the lack of three square meals a day growing up had been the least of her problems.

The sheriff reached across the seat and tapped her elbow to pull her attention from her thoughts. He pointed to an imposing building with a gray brick and white stone facade on the corner at the end of the street. "There's your hotel. Used to be a mining office, but now it's completely remodeled inside. Want to check in first?"

Alarmed to realize her thoughts kept drifting to the past instead of focusing squarely on her present assignment, Joanna resolutely straightened in her seat. "Let's go directly to your office. I want to familiarize myself with my surroundings before I meet the suspect I'm interrogating."

"You want the home field advantage?" he teased.

"Something like that." They had almost driven out of the far edge of town before Joanna spotted the rambling four-story building with signs that read Kenner City Sheriff and Kenner County Crime Unit. "I read the file from Supervisor Ortiz, but I'd like to get your take on things since you've worked more closely on Agent Grainger's murder. What can you tell me about your suspect, Sherman Watts?"

Good. She got the name out without so much as a stutter of hesitation.

Focus on the job, Joanna. Watts is just a job.

"He's a local troublemaker. Been convicted and jailed on any number of petty crimes—mostly drunk and disorderly, a couple of assaults."

"A-assault?" *That* was a definite hesitation.

But Martinez, fortunately, didn't pick up on the way she stiffened in her seat. He pulled into a slanted parking space in front of the building. "When Watts is drunk, he can get mean."

So some things never changed in Kenner County. "You don't have him in custody?"

"We suspect he's been doing odd jobs for the Nicky Wayne crime family out of Vegas, like helping Wayne's hit man, Boyd Perkins, hide out in the area. However, what we believe and what we can prove are two different things. That's why he's still a free man. But he's definitely a person of interest we've been watching. Could be he had nothing to do with the murder, and he's only funneling information to them—someone sure seems to be."

She'd heard about the information leaks that had dogged the investigation, seeming to give Boyd Perkins—the man reputed to have killed mob boss Vincent Del Gardo, as well as the bureau's chief suspect in Agent Grainger's murder—a heads-up when to go into hiding or carry out another attack. "How do you want me to direct my interrogation? Confirm the source of the security leak? Find out if Perkins is still in the area and pinpoint his location? Or should I concentrate on Watts himself, and tie him to Boyd Perkins and Agent Grainger's murder so you can make an arrest?"

"Anything you can get out of him. I don't make him for premeditated murder—I'd be surprised if he has the backbone for that. But I wouldn't put it past him to hurt someone if he felt threatened."

She didn't need to read the Kenner County Crime Unit—KCCU, according to her mission brief—report to know his assessment of Sherman Watts was on the money. Drunk or sober—if that ever happened—the fifty-eight-year-old Indian was as dangerous and unpredictable as a badger. If he got cornered, he was just as likely to turn and attack as he was to skulk away into some hole. If he felt he was entitled to something, he'd take it—as long as he thought he could get away with it. And damn to anyone who tried to stop him.

"You owe me, bitch."

With her face smashed down into the bed and his heavy weight on top of her, Joanna's screams were muffled. The wool lint from the blankets filtered into her nose and mouth with each gasp, and she could scarcely breathe.

He'd hit her hard enough, too, to make the room spin. But the pain was clear, the humiliation intense. Oh, God, it hurt. Right down to her soul, it hurt.

Son of a bitch. Joanna jerked her mind back to the rain and the sheriff and the present, and forced herself to breathe. So she had a little extra insight into Sherman Watts and how his mind worked. That's what criminal profiling was all about, right? Knowing the truth about the suspect—knowing his secrets—could only help her get this interview done more quickly and efficiently.

Joanna pried her fingers off the armrest to unbuckle her seat belt. She breathed deeply, clearly, in through her nose and out through her mouth, more determined than ever to leave the past in the past so she could help Martinez and his people deal with the present. "Is there any hard evidence to connect Watts to Julie Grainger's murder? Any motive?"

Either unaware of her momentary discomfort, or politely ignoring it, the sheriff continued. "We know that Agent Grainger was on the trail of fifty million dollars that crime boss Vincent Del Gardo hid in the area. If she found it, or had a clue on her that would lead to its location, then that's fifty million reasons why just about anybody would want to kill her. One of our lab teams found a leather necklace that we believe belonged to

Watts at the site where her body was dumped. That puts him at the scene—before or after her death, though, we don't know."

"You think Watts has the fifty mil?"

"No. Someone's still looking for it, or the attacks would have stopped." Martinez muttered a curse, clearly frustrated with the lack of closure on the case. His eyes were clear glacial blue when they locked on to hers. "Sherman Watts is a survivor. He'll do whatever it takes to stay alive and stay one step ahead of us. There was a time when Watts would pick a fight at one of the local bars, just so he could spend a warm night in jail. Now he's living in a new trailer on the rez and drinking name-brand booze. He claims his money is from an inheritance. I haven't been able to prove otherwise."

"You don't believe him."

He shook his head. "Nicky Wayne and his family have laundered enough money that they could make it look as if Watts's income is from a legitimate source. If they're funding him, Watts may be uncatchable right now."

Letting Watts get away with aiding and abetting, theft, murder—or God knew what—wasn't going to happen. Never again. "I'll get him in a room and get him to talk. I'll find out what he knows."

Martinez nodded, believing the strength of her words. "I've sent a couple of men out to the reservation to bring him in for questioning."

She waved aside the offer of an umbrella, retrieved her bag and followed him inside.

He nodded to the security guard reading a newspaper at the front desk and led Joanna past him to a reception area at the center of a suite of offices. "Anybody home?" Martinez hollered. He removed his hat and knocked it against his leg before brushing away the moisture beading on the shoulders of his black tux jacket. "Elizabeth?"

Joanna frowned, smoothing the damp hair around her face as she surveyed the executive office area and the hallways, elevator and doors branching off in either direction. "I was led to believe this was a fully staffed facility. Where is everyone?"

"Like I said, we had a wedding this afternoon. Our chief forensic scientist, Dr. Calista MacBride, married Tom Ryan. Tom's been with us as an FBI investigator almost from the day I first saw Julie Grainger's body. I guess the two of them went through the academy together—Tom and Julie, that is. I think Tom and Callie were, uh…friends, if you know what I mean, even before the murder brought them back together." He turned toward the locker rooms and staff entrance at the end of the hall. "Elizabeth? You here yet?"

Joanna noted the name plate on the high front counter at the center of the carpeted waiting area. She dismissed the sudden chill of remembrance as the rain trickled down the back of her scalp. This Tom and Callie weren't the only old friends to be reunited by this case. "Elizabeth Reddawn is your receptionist?"

The sheriff set his hat on the counter beside the nameplate. "You know her?"

"Old friend" wasn't exactly the right term. Joanna's parents, Ralph and Naomi, had alienated most of the decent people she knew by the time they'd died in a drunk-driving accident when she was eighteen. And once Joanna had left for college and her career, she'd never looked back. Until now. Yet there were bound to be harder memories to face than this one. She would handle them all. Supervisor Ortiz and her boss back in Washington, D.C., were counting on her. "I grew up on the rez over in Mesa Ridge. Elizabeth worked for the reservation sheriff back then."

"Elmer Watts?"

Probably the man Martinez had replaced when the county and reservation units had merged. Sherman Watts's uncle. Joanna nodded.

Elizabeth had been the only one in that office who'd really listened to Joanna when she'd needed their help. But as a lowly secretary, Elizabeth Reddawn had been as powerless as Joanna had been. And the resulting pity she'd offered had been no help at all.

"Then this will be a reunion of sorts for you."

"I suppose."

Martinez gestured toward the door marked Sheriff. "Let me make a couple of calls to see where my people are." After setting her bag behind the reception counter, he turned back to Joanna. His smile faded and she caught a glimpse of the sharp, protective-of-his-own man in charge Supervisor Ortiz had described. "Don't pass judgment on my team, Agent Rhodes. They can all use a break for one afternoon. This has been one twisted case and we've taken some personal hits that haven't gone down real well. We lost crucial evidence during that blizzard back in March. I've had a witness with amnesia and a crime boss who was killed before he could give me any answers. Our families have been attacked—my people tested in every way imaginable. The lab has gathered plenty of evidence and we've all got our suspicions, but we need to tie the pieces together and make it stick. We need somebody behind bars. Soon."

"Of course, sir." Her acquiescence seemed to appease the protective papa-bear growl of his voice. "I'm here to work—not catch up with former acquaintances."

"In my head, I know you're not the enemy. Still, it feels like a slap in the face for the bureau to bring in a big gun from outside our investigation to get us over this stone wall we've run into." He pulled back the front of his jacket and propped his hands near the gun and badge at his waist. "I guess I can see the bureau's logic in bringing in a Native American to interview Watts. I suppose he's more likely to respond to one of his own."

One of his own? Joanna's skin crawled at the comparison.

But she didn't so much as bat an eyelash. "Possibly."

So not only was she coming into a tightly knit group of co-workers, but Martinez was hinting that there was resentment against her being here. Joanna was used to being the odd man out. As the daughter of Ralph and Naomi Kuchu, she'd grown up not fitting in with normal families who worked hard and paid their bills and protected their children.

Since the day of her parents' funeral, she'd taken that loner persona and turned it into a strength. She was trained to be courteous and professional right down to her painted pinkie toe, but she'd discovered that if she remained dispassionate and in control she was harder to read. And if the bad guy sitting across the interview table from her couldn't get into her head, then he had no advantage over her.

No one had an advantage over her if she didn't let them in.

"I'm not here to mop up any mess or steal any thunder from your people, Sheriff. The bureau just wants vindication for the murder of one of their own." She could handle the isolation, but if Martinez's team resented her enough to actually work against her, then they'd have no chance of success. "Perhaps I should clarify the kind of support I'll need from you."

"Yeah?"

Simple. "All I need is a room, and Watts. If he knows anything, I'll get you the information you need. You're welcome to make any arrests or pursue any leads that might result. I'm just a tool the bureau is providing your investigation. Use me."

Martinez nodded, accepting the arrangement. For now. She could see he still had his suspicions about her motivation for being here. "Ortiz says you're up for a big promotion back in D.C."

No point in lying about that. "If I don't deliver here, they may reconsider."

"This is a test for you, eh?"

More than anyone here or in D.C. would ever know. "Yes."

Any hint of western hospitality disappeared as he leaned in and issued a warning. "I won't have your career ambitions get in the way of my case or jeopardize the safety of my team. Are we clear on that?"

Joanna stood as tall and straight as her dignity and two-inch heels allowed. "Yes, sir. I won't let you down."

He pulled back, relaxing his shoulders if not quite smiling again. "Good. I'll go make those calls and find some people."

"Don't bother, Patrick." A squat woman with a thick black bun on the back of her head waddled into the reception area. She peeled a clear plastic rain slicker off her scarlet blouse and brightly patterned skirt, hanging the coat up beside the reception counter as she talked. "We're on our way back. Since they're only taking the weekend off, I think Callie and Tom are anxious to get their honeymoon started, so the festivities are breaking up." The sixtyish petite woman turned her eyes, dark as night but shining with laughter, up to Joanna. She clapped her hands together. "As I live and breathe. Joanna?"

"Good to see you again, Elizabeth."

"'Good to see…'?" She tutted. "What kind of greeting is that?" Elizabeth Reddawn flung her arms open and squeezed Joanna against her ample bosom. "My goodness, child, how you've grown up."

The woman's enthusiastic welcome seemed to demand some kind of a response before she'd let go. Nonplussed by the effusive human contact she typically avoided, Joanna finally reached around and patted the back of the older woman's shoulders, completing the hug. "It's been fifteen years."

"Has it really?" Elizabeth pulled away, her eyes crinkling with the depth of her smile. She maintained a clasp on Joanna's fingers, alerting her that there was more personal conversation to come, even though she turned away and tilted her head toward the sheriff. "By the way, Patrick? Bree asked if you still wanted to do a movie with her and Charlie tonight because they'd stay in town instead of going home."

"Are you kidding? That new action-hero movie opens tonight. Of course I'm taking my son." He turned to include Joanna in a wink that erased his stern countenance. "Bree would be the wife. She gets to hold the popcorn and keep Charlie and me in line." He nodded to Elizabeth. "You'll keep our guest company for a few minutes?"

"Of course."

"Excuse me."

"So…" Turning her maternal indulgence from the sheriff's retreating back to Joanna, Elizabeth took hold of both hands and quickly inspected her from head to toe. "Joanna Kuchu—Daughter of the Buffalo. You've matured into a woman as beautiful and powerful as your namesake."

As Elizabeth pulled her toward the couch and chairs of the seating area, Joanna gently disengaged her hands. "It's Joanna Rhodes now."

Elizabeth sat and patted the sofa cushion beside her. "You're married?"

"No." Joanna perched on the edge of the couch, curling her fingers into her lap. "I was a Rhodes scholar my senior year at Yale. I liked the name—I liked the honor—so I had it legally changed."

"I see." Her quizzical frown indicated she suspected there were deeper reasons for erasing her past. However, the Elizabeth Reddawn Joanna remembered wouldn't have pried unless invited to do so—even if she was champing at the bit to ask questions. Judging by the way she kept plucking at her wool skirt, the older woman was definitely itching to ask something. But Joanna wasn't offering. "That's wonderful. Congratulations."

"Thanks." Several silent moments passed, leaving Joanna wondering how long Martinez would be on the phone to his wife, and how long she could sit here smiling and pretending that this reunion wasn't awkward as hell for her. "How do you like working for Sheriff Martinez and the crime lab?"

"It's nicer than working at old Elmer's office ever was. And I'm not just talking about the new furniture and state-of-the-art facilities in our lab." Despite Joanna's stiff posture, Elizabeth reached across and squeezed her hand around one of the fists in her lap. "These are good people here. You'll like them."

The other woman's caring touch seeped into Joanna's fingers and shot little tendrils of distracting warmth into her resolve to stay focused solely on work while she was in Kenner City. "I'm only here for a couple of days. I doubt I'll have time to get to know them."

"What about the people in Kenner City and Mesa Ridge you already…? Oh. Of course." Elizabeth politely pulled away, no doubt sensing the protective personal barriers Joanna was pushing back into place. "I don't suppose you have relatives in the area to keep you here."

"No."

"Will you be paying your respects to your mother and daddy?"

"Hadn't planned on it."

"Ethan Bia has been back in town for a few years now, after his stint in the army."

Ethan Bia? A shiver of recognition, of feelings long buried and often regretted, danced along Joanna's spine.

She flashed through the remembered sensations of a young man's eager touch—the patient demands of his mouth on her untutored lips. She blotted out the image of anger she'd seen only once on his tanned, rugged face—the last memory she had of the gentle giant she'd once loved.

"Ethan left Mesa Ridge?" That was almost more surprising than her reaction to the mere mention of his name.

Elizabeth jumped on the question. "For six years. He's a consultant with the crime lab now. Works search and rescue in the area. What about calling him—?"

"I'm not here to socialize."

Joanna hardened herself against the name, as warring memories of strength and warmth, regret and shame, surged inside her.

"Nüa-rü. *The wind.*" *He stroked the long strand of hair off her face and tucked it behind her ear. "You're just as elusive to me."*

"Ethan…"

She'd had to leave. Just as surely as Ethan had had to stay. He was tied to the earth and the mountains in a way she'd never been tied to anything or anyone.

A smack across the face. A knife at her breast.

"You owe me, bitch."

Joanna jerked inside her skin. No. No way could she have stayed.

"Honey?" Elizabeth's hand was on hers again.

The locker-room doors swung open, thankfully putting an end to the discomfort of reacquainting herself with the past.

"Madre de Dios," muttered one Latino man, shaking

the rain from his black hair. "It hasn't let up once since noon. It'll be raining buckets by sunset."

"You're telling me."

Joanna pushed to her feet as a second man—same height, same black hair, same features save for the scar that bisected his chin—came up beside him. Both wore suits, although the first one was already pulling off his tie and stuffing it into his pocket as they approached.

The second one pulled a cell phone from his belt beside the gun he wore. "I'd better give Aspen a call at school and tell her I'll pick up Jack from the sitter's. I don't want her on those muddy reservation back roads any more than necessary. I predict a washout in our future. No pun intended."

"Nice one, *hermano*." The first one elbowed his buddy in the arm. "Emma talked about seeing great waters and danger in her dreams last night."

"Maybe she should take up weather forecasting."

"Yeah, and maybe you should call your wife before she forgets what you look like. Again."

"Ouch." Both men laughed as they moved their magnets on the sign-in board behind the reception counter to indicate that they were back in the office and on duty. "Point taken. I'll leave the one-liners to you."

Joanna didn't need Elizabeth mouthing the word "twins" to recognize the resemblance. She didn't particularly need the nudge forward as Elizabeth insisted on introducing them, either. "Miguel? Dylan? I'd like you to meet the daughter of an old friend of mine, Joanna Kuch—" She caught the mistake. "Joanna Rhodes. She'll be working with us for a few days."

Extending her hand in a professional greeting,

Joanna completed the introductions herself. She'd done her homework. "Agent Dylan Acevedo. Supervisor Ortiz told me you'd transferred here because you were friends with the deceased, Agent Grainger."

"Julie and I went through the academy together— along with Tom Ryan and Ben Parrish. We've all been working the case." Dylan—the one with the scar— shook her hand, nodding toward the badge at her waist. "You're FBI?"

"I'm with the D.C. office. Profiling and interrogation specialist. I'm here to interview Sherman Watts."

Dylan's twin shook her hand next. "Good luck with that one. He's a wily SOB. The man's got nine lives when it comes to staying ahead of the law. I'm Miguel Acevedo."

Joanna recognized the name. "You're a crime-scene investigator with the forensic lab."

"That's right." He unbuttoned the collar of his shirt and shucked his jacket, looking like a man who was anxious to get out of his wedding apparel and get back to work. "So you're the big gun Martinez said the bureau was bringing in to crack this case for us."

You don't have to make friends, she reminded herself. *You just have to get the job done.* Her promotion and the ability to walk away from here emotionally unscathed depended on it. "That's my intention. The information in the case file that KCCU prepared for me was very thorough. I'm sure it will be invaluable to the success of my interview."

The locker-room door opened again at the end of the hall. She needn't have worried about the laxness or scarcity of the staff. This wasn't the reservation sheriff's office of fifteen years ago. She was beginning to believe the paperwork she'd read. The KCCU was a diverse, dedicated staff of scientists and area law enforcement. The blond-haired man strolling toward them appeared to be no exception.

He walked straight up to Joanna and the Acevedos and diffused the tension between them by leaning down to kiss Elizabeth's cheek. "Lizzie, you left the reception before that dance you promised me. Broke my heart."

"Oh, Ben." She swatted at his arm. "I'm a married woman."

"All the good ones are taken, hmm?"

Elizabeth blushed at the flirtation from a much younger man.

He grinned as he straightened to introduce himself. "Ben Parrish, FBI."

"Joanna Rhodes, the same."

She noted that his handsome smile didn't quite reach his wary eyes. "Don't let these guys give you any grief. I was the new kid here myself a few months back. Now I've grown on them."

"Like a fungus, Parrish," Miguel teased. "I'd better change and get up to the lab. With Callie taking a couple of days off, I want to make sure we've got everything covered and on schedule for the weekend." His smile seemed genuine enough as he excused himself. "If there's anything you need from the lab, Agent Rhodes, let me know."

"Thank you."

As his brother pushed open the stairwell door and jogged up the stairs, Dylan Acevedo toned his indignation at an outsider's interference down to an I'll-wait-to-pass-judgment-once-I-see-what-kind-of-job-you-can-do status. "Watts and his buddy Perkins have already gone after my wife and Miguel's. One or both of them are responsible for other attacks in the area. I'm guessing Sheriff Martinez already told you we make Boyd Perkins for Julie's murder. There's not a one of us who doesn't want to put him away. If you can help us find the bastard…"

"I'll get what your team needs out of Watts, Agent Acevedo," Joanna reassured him. "And you're welcome to make the arrest."

"What do you get out of this?" Miguel asked.

"Miguel!" Elizabeth chided.

Telling him this was about a promotion wouldn't build any trust. Telling him her personal reasons for accepting this assignment wasn't an option, either. Joanna settled for a truth somewhere in between. "The satisfaction of a job well-done."

"We can all use a little of that," Ben intervened. Joanna nodded, appreciating his support more than she realized. She didn't have to worry about thanking him, though. He turned away to mark himself In on the duty board and nodded for Miguel to follow him into an office opposite the sheriff's. "I want you to tell me more about that medal Julie sent you before she died. There has to be a reason why you, me and Tom all got one."

Once the door closed on their conversation, Joanna became aware of the warmth of Elizabeth Reddawn's hand, still linked through the crook of her elbow. Had the older woman been holding on to her this entire time? Claiming her as a friend? Subtly hanging on in the face of the teasing, doubt and outright resentment from the three men?

As uncomfortable with the show of support as she was unaccustomed to it, Joanna shrugged away from Elizabeth's touch. She busied her fingers, plucking imaginary specks from her blazer and slacks. She was perfectly capable of standing on her own two feet in this investigation without the older woman's help. Joanna just needed a moment to shore up her defenses again, make sure her powers of observation, her strength and intellect, were firmly in place. "Could you show me where the interview rooms are? I'm afraid Sheriff Martinez has been held up on the phone."

"Sure, hon." Elizabeth's frown indicated disappointment at Joanna's abrupt insistence on working rather than resuming their trip down memory lane. But there was also something she supposed was maternal understanding when she patted Joanna's arm. "Come on around this way. There are two rooms, with an observation window in between." Elizabeth led her back toward the security desk and a hallway that ran parallel to this wing of offices. "Can I get you some coffee?"

"Black, thanks. That would be lovely."

"I'll brew a fresh pot and bring it right in."

As Elizabeth bustled away, Joanna paused for a moment to inhale a quieting breath. But she'd switched on the light in the first room before realizing how much Elizabeth Reddawn and the secrets from the reservation they shared had gotten into her head and diverted her focus from the investigation.

"You forgot the case file, Sherlock." Stopping short of thumping herself on the forehead, Joanna retraced her steps. She'd already mapped out her strategy for questioning Watts. Now she needed to choreograph her questions with the placement of chairs and where she would sit or stand during each phase of the interview.

Joanna unzipped her bag and pulled out the thick manila envelope with the case reports and her notes. She'd just acknowledged the security guard in the lobby when the front door opened with a rush of wind and patter of raindrops.

"Elizabeth?" The familiar male voice swept straight through her, mocking any attempt to keep her emotions in check. "You left your purse at the church. What are you carrying in this thing, bricks?"

Joanna stopped in her tracks. Stared.

The man, easily six foot four, froze in the open doorway. His dark eyes narrowed as they locked on to hers. The wind glued his brown suit jacket to his broad shoulders. The rain made his military-short hair glisten like polished onyx.

"Joanna?" The timbre of his voice darkened. The deep pitch of it filled up his chest and rumbled out in a seductive whisper.

"Ethan." Here. In the flesh. Impossibly bigger, broader, harder than the man she remembered. The silent intensity of his dark, nearly black eyes hit her like a sucker punch to the heart.

Ethan Bia.

The man she'd given her virginity and her young girl's heart to.

The man who'd taught her how to survive the mountains—and her family.

The man she'd walked away from fifteen years ago without ever looking back.

Chapter Two

"What are you doing here?" Ethan asked, anchoring his boots to the floor and holding himself still against the impulse leaping through every muscle of his body. Fly across the room and scoop her up in a fierce hug.

But another part of him had grown wiser and more cautious over the years. One, they had an audience in the form of Officer Bates at the security desk. And two, even if they were all alone, he wasn't too keen on getting his ego smacked or his heart crushed again.

He'd seen plenty of death and destruction in his years as an army ranger and his two tours of duty in Afghanistan. He'd dealt with loss in his work as a search-and-rescue team leader. But nothing had ever hit him as hard or left him feeling as powerless as watching Joanna Kuchu's tearstained face when she'd scrambled out of his truck that last warm spring night on the rez.

"There are no good memories for me here. I have the chance to leave and I'm taking it. Goodbye, Ethan."

She was barely eighteen and he was only twenty-one, but he'd known in his bones that they were supposed to last.

But boom. They were done. She was gone.

And he was the man left behind.

"I'm working the Julie Grainger murder investigation," she explained, clutching a thick investigation file against her chest. Her fingers fiddled with the edge of the manila envelope in a subtle revelation of nerves. But they stilled almost as soon as he noticed the unconscious movement.

Always guarded, always with a plan, always thinking two or three steps ahead of everyone else in the room. That part of her personality hadn't changed.

"I knew there was a good chance I'd run into you. We should get this meeting over with so that it doesn't cost either of us more pain than it has to." She pointed over his shoulder. "You're getting wet and so's the rug. Why don't you close the door? I'm sure we can find a private place to talk."

No good memories. Not even him. Them. She'd been through hell those last few months—and the years before hadn't been much better, so he'd never held her need to leave against her. But she'd never even let him try to help. She'd refused his offer to go with her. And his love hadn't been enough for her to stay.

Ethan pushed the door shut behind him. He might not hold her obsessive drive to escape Mesa Ridge and the reservation against her. Didn't mean he had to let her fillet his heart open and char it over the flames of false hope and misguided passion again, either.

"I'm just here to deliver this to a friend," he explained, holding up the purse he carried.

"Elizabeth?" She inclined her head toward the main hallway, exposing a swanlike expanse of neck that beckoned to randy memories from the past. "She's in the break room making coffee. I'll walk you back."

Though this sure as hell wasn't the homecoming he'd once wished for, spending a few impersonal minutes in her company could no longer hurt him. Ethan shortened his stride and fell into step beside her. "Time has treated you well."

"You look good, too." She arched an eyebrow and gave him a glimpse of the hesitant smile he remembered. "Your hair's a lot shorter. And you—" her long, agile fingers gestured in the air "—filled out. Got big. You're taller and broader both, it looks like to me."

More than six years of elite army training and service, plus the rugged outdoorsman life he led, did that to a man. "I guess."

"How's Kyle?"

It made sense that she'd ask about his younger brother. They'd been classmates and good friends. Of course, she and Ethan had been so much more than friends, but she didn't need him to point that out. "He's good. Married. Two kids. Lives in Cortez now."

"Still a man of few words, I see."

"No sense wasting them." Stopping at Elizabeth Reddawn's desk, Ethan set down the purse and unhooked his collar and loosened the black string tie he wore, silently assessing the changes in Joanna's appearance as she turned to face him.

Despite the warmth of her olive complexion and dark brown eyes, there was a brittleness to her ramrod posture and polite words. He idly wondered if a stroke of his fingertip across the nape of her neck could still make her shiver, or if the touch of his lips against hers could break through those invisible barriers she wore like body armor and unleash the warmth and softness and eagerness to explore her own sexuality he remembered.

The black-as-midnight hair she'd pulled back into a sleek ponytail was shorter than the wild horse's tail of a hairdo she'd worn through high school. She'd grown, too. Maybe it was the high heels she was wearing—he'd never seen those on her feet before—but the top of her head was just about even with his chin now. The curve of her lips sported a sheer berry tint that hadn't been there fifteen years ago, and her tailored suit was a far cry from the jeans and tees she'd lived in back then. The beautiful woman standing in front of him looked as polished and businesslike and cold as the gun holstered at her waist.

The curious, coltish tomboy who'd tagged along with him and his younger brother, Kyle, on their adventures around the reservation had vanished. The years apart had erased the young woman with the shy sensuality and big dreams whom he'd patiently coaxed into loving and trusting him. Pity there was no sign of the fire within that had once drawn him like a moth to a flame.

But idle thoughts were as useless as idle words.

"You're FBI?" he asked.

She nodded. "I made it into the program at Quantico after graduating with my master's in psychology. Made it all the way to Washington, D.C., where I'm assigned now as a behavioral scientist and criminal profiler."

"Good." That was what she'd wanted—to move East, to put the entire country between her and the memories of her parents' deaths and the compounding tragedy that followed. She'd longed for urban landscapes and busy, diverse city streets instead of the endless red-rock terrain and isolation of the reservation and the small mountain towns like Mesa Ridge and Kenner City. She'd wanted to carry a gun and take down bad guys and give the victims like herself, who'd been denied a voice, a champion who could save the day. She'd wanted things he couldn't give her. "Congratulations."

"Thanks."

So she'd finally gotten what she wanted. On some noble level, he was happy for her. But deeper down, somewhere between his battered heart and old man's soul, it had always felt like unfinished business between them—as though fate and her stubborn will had seen fit to deny them the wonderful possibilities of loving each other.

Just punishment, Ethan supposed. He hadn't protected her well enough back then—hadn't even sensed how badly she'd needed his protection until it was too late. He'd been more interested in getting in her pants and making her see the world—and their future together—through his eyes.

Yeah. More than anyone he knew, Joanna Kuchu deserved to have her dreams come true. Even if those dreams didn't include him. He was glad that she'd finally found her place in the world.

After moving on for a while, he'd come to realize that he was already where he needed to be. He'd come home from that last hellish deployment to the land whose spirit flowed through him like his own blood. He needed the open space and quiet the way she needed the bustle and technology and new faces around every turn in the big city.

When the silence stretched on long enough for her coffee-dark gaze to drop to the middle of his chest, Ethan knew there was no sense prolonging their would've-could've-should've-been reunion. He smoothed his hand over the top of his cropped hair and down the back of his scalp, taking away a palmful of dampness with it. There was no good way to let this woman go. He just had to do it. "I hope life always gives you what you need, Jo."

Her dark eyes flinched and darted back up to his. "You, too, Ethan. You're kinder than I deserve. I'm…" Those berry lips tightened into a frown that tugged at both his heart and conscience. "I'm—"

"I know." He knew the sentiment by heart. "You're sorry. So am I." Before he could act on the impulse to take her in his arms to trade comforts and remind his body what hers felt like pressed against it, he pointed to the overstuffed bag he'd set on the counter. "Would you make sure Elizabeth gets this?"

"Of course."

Ethan turned, ending the conversation and walking away. He needed the rain on his face to cool his skin along with the desire and regrets simmering just beneath the surface. He needed a long, fast drive into the countryside and a hike up into the mountains to put behind him his feelings for Joanna and the damnable understanding he had for why the two of them could never work.

"Goodbye, Ethan."

Those dream-destroying words grated against his ears. Fifteen years and that woman could still get to him. Must be the guilt. *Keep walking, buddy. You can't change the past.* He pushed open the door.

"Agent Rhodes?" Patrick Martinez's voice echoed

through the reception area behind him. "I finished those calls. My men are en route to pick up the suspect."

Agent *Rhodes?* Ethan glanced over his shoulder and scanned for the second person his sharp eyes wouldn't have missed. Wariness seeped up through the soles of his boots and put him on alert.

"Hey, Ethan." Martinez acknowledged him with a nod as he strode up beside Joanna. "You coming or going?"

Turning, Ethan quickly accounted for every person here. Joanna. Martinez. Bates. *She* had to be Agent Rhodes. What was going on here?

His eyes swept Joanna from head to toe, coming back twice to her bare left hand as she tucked Elizabeth's purse behind the counter. He hadn't even considered the idea that she'd gotten married. That she might find someone else after leaving him.

He hadn't. No one that ever stuck in his heart the way she had, at any rate.

The idea that another man had been able to give her what he couldn't burned through him.

But any questions about new names and old relationships remained unspoken at the sheriff's next words. "If you want to step into my office, I can spare a few minutes now to go over any other questions you might have regarding Sherman Watts."

The current of awareness that flowed from the earth into Ethan's body blazed into a full-blown warning. "What does she have to do with Sherman Watts?"

Joanna's ponytail bobbed against her neck as she gave him a quick shake of her head. *Not a word,* she silently pleaded.

So much for the ice in her eyes.

Martinez didn't know her history with Watts? The FBI was allowing this?

No. He could see it in her face. She hadn't told them.

"Would you excuse us a minute, Patrick?" Ignoring every vow to keep his distance, Ethan clamped his fingers around Joanna's arm and ushered her into the nearest open room he could find. Though her sinewy muscles twisted beneath his grip, he never let go. And she never muttered a sound that might indicate to the sheriff that she was moving against her will.

"You two know each other?" Patrick called after them. "Well, ain't that a surprise."

Ethan ignored the amusement he heard in his friend's tone and pushed Joanna into an empty interview room. He closed the door, releasing her. "What do you think you're doing?"

He blocked the exit with his body as she stormed across the room and came back in a useless attempt to get past him. The file crumpled in her grasp as she tilted her chin to glare in defiance. "You already asked me that. I'm working the Julie Grainger murder. Now move. I have a briefing with the sheriff."

She knew better than to play stupid with him. He rephrased the question. "Why are you messing with Watts?"

"My assignment is to interview him."

"Get someone else."

"Never a man to mince words, are you, Ethan?"

"He raped you."

Her skin blanched beneath her tan. The fire in her eyes went out as her chin dropped and her hazy focus landed on the middle button of his creased white shirt. He felt like a bastard playing the voice of reason here, but someone had to make her see how badly she could be hurt if she went head to head with Sherman Watts again.

The bruises and blood and violation had been bad enough when he'd found her at her trailer that night after her parents' funeral. But the emotional toll had been even more devastating. That night had killed her warmth. Killed her trust. Killed her love for him. He didn't ever want to see her suffer like that again. If she wouldn't protect herself from facing that unrepentant monster, then by damn, he'd do it for her.

Her deep, stuttering breath broke the silence of the room, reminding him to move past his raging emotions and seek out that calming sense of quiet inside himself again. She wasn't a man under his command, and he shouldn't be barking orders to get his point across.

"Joanna—" He reached for her pale cheek, but she knocked his hand away, the same way she had that night.

"Do you think that's something I can forget?" Her gaze briefly touched his before she turned away to dump the file on the table opposite the observation window. Keeping his feet rooted to the spot, Ethan watched her take a moment to smooth a straight strand of hair off her face and pull her shoulders back. By the time she faced him again, that prickly, polite chill was back in place. "This isn't about revenge."

"Bull."

"The statute of limitations ran out on my assault before anything could be proved, so there's no longer a conflict of interest for me to work this case. I've accepted that he'll never pay for what he did to me."

"I haven't."

His stark, growly pronouncement seemed to take her

aback. He watched the muscles travel down her long neck as she swallowed hard before speaking. "The attack wasn't your fault, Ethan."

"I should have been there."

"I told you I needed some time alone that day. You were giving me the space I needed after Mom and Dad's funeral. If I'd known he still had feelings for Mom…"

Her fingers clenched at her side and he got the feeling she was fighting back the urge to reach out to him, as well.

"What happened afterward—Watts's never even being arrested—that wasn't your fault, either."

Didn't make Watts any less of a bullying bastard who'd gotten away with crap his entire life because of who he was related to. Didn't make Ethan feel any more like a man who'd done right by the girl he loved, either. "He can still hurt you. In ways you may not even have imagined yet."

"I've imagined all of them," was her stark answer. "But this is my job."

"Go back to D.C. This is too personal."

Joanna laced her fingers together and tapped her knuckles against her lips, thinking for a moment before she slowly began to pace. She seemed to choose each and every word with laser-beam precision. "I'll concede that I won't lose any sleep if Watts is arrested for a different crime. That's not why I'm here. I didn't volunteer for this assignment, but I didn't argue when it was given to me, either. If I can't face whatever criminal I run up against—even my own rapist—over an interview table, then I'm not tough enough to do this job.

"Make no mistake, there's a reward involved if I prove to myself I can do this. If I break this case—if I can break Watts—I'm guaranteed a promotion in D.C. and I'll never have to come back to this place again." She stopped in front of him, her hands curled into fists as she faced him once more. "I know that sounds cold and calculating, but this is what I do. This is what I *need* to do. I'm the go-to woman who's going to get Watts to talk. He'll tell me who murdered Agent Grainger, and maybe where that fifty million dollars of Vincent Del Gardo's is hidden. Besting him at *my* game will be justice enough for me."

Pulling back his jacket, Ethan propped his hands at his waist, shaking his head at her misguided plan. "I don't want you alone in the same room with him."

"Isn't it fortunate, then, that it's not your decision to make?"

She retrieved her folder, tucked it under her arm and walked up to him as though she thought he would simply move aside. Screw this. Ethan reached out to lightly pinch the upturned point of her chin between his thumb and forefinger. She stiffened for a moment. But when she didn't pull away and the warm coffee of her eyes stayed locked on to his gaze, he traced the line of her jaw, rediscovering the softness of her skin.

"Don't do this, sweetheart."

"Ethan…" She squeezed her eyes shut against the stroke of his hand, pressing her lips into a thin line to block the words and emotions locked up behind them.

"Shh." He rubbed his thumb across the tight frown, urging her muscles to relax. He swept his fingertips lightly across her cheek.

When she turned her face into the caress, something cracked open inside him—his need for a woman to warm his bed, perhaps, or maybe the memories of how this particular woman had once enjoyed his touch. Her timid response took him back in time, when her long legs had caught his eye, and her innocence had captured his soul. Touching Joanna like this made him feel things, want things that weren't his to ask for anymore. He tunneled his fingers beneath the heavy silk of her ponytail and let his broad palm cup the length of her neck. He leaned in, touched his forehead to hers and whispered, "You're not as tough as you act. You weren't fifteen years ago and you aren't now."

Her eyes popped open and looked straight up into his. "Fifteen years can change a person, Ethan." She braced her hand against his chest and gently pushed him away. "I haven't been that teenage girl who had a crush on my best friend's big brother for a long time."

He'd been more than a crush, and she wasn't the only one who'd changed during their time apart. But neither comment seemed to mean much right now. She wasn't here to recapture the relationship that had been, and he wouldn't force her into the relationship that could be. Not when she was so intent on leaving. Again.

As he disentangled his fingers from her hair, he let her nudge him aside. Joanna patted the spot on his chest, then curled her fingers into her palm. It was a kind, but definite, send-off. "I have a new name, a new life. You don't know me anymore."

Ethan stayed in the small room for a moment as the door opened and closed. He listened to the spirit of Mother Earth inside him, listened to his training as a soldier, listened to his conscience—and made a decision. He opened the door and followed her out.

Joanna Kuchu—make that Rhodes now—didn't know him, either, if she thought he was going to let her face off against that bastard Watts on her own a second time.

"GET IT TOGETHER, GIRL," Joanna muttered. The skin at her nape was still tingling with tiny tremors from the warmth of Ethan's hand.

Her heart pounded away at an equally unsettling rate as she left the interview room and forced one foot in front of the other along the KCCU's tiled hallway. She could do this. She *had* to do this. She'd prepared herself to look Sherman Watts in the eye, to see familiar faces and places and deal with the memories they might trigger.

But she hadn't prepared herself for Ethan Bia.

Not really.

She'd forgotten how impossible it was to reason with him—how he could watch her with those dark, nearly black, eyes and get under her skin and into her head and make her think that *she* was the one who was being unreasonable. His inner peace and age-old wisdom—even at twenty-one—had frustrated her as much as it fascinated. His certainty about the world and belief in what was right or wrong had confounded as much as it had comforted her. He'd been a rock in her chaotic young life, a constant she'd never known with her alcoholic parents. He'd also been a mysterious, compelling—completely sexy man.

Maybe that was the part she hadn't prepared herself for.

Stopping to straighten her jacket and tuck her hair back into place, Joanna gave herself a moment to silence the confusion in her head. She'd devoted herself to her career, taught herself that her strongest allies were her own wits and determination. She'd gone through counseling and had prepared herself to accept a man's touch again. It wasn't so much that she was afraid of being with a man at some point in the future, but that she was afraid of needing him.

Ethan Bia, with that deep, rumbly voice and those gentle, work-roughened hands, had undone in fifteen minutes what had taken her fifteen years to firmly fix into place.

He'd gotten her blood boiling with his insistence that she had no business working an investigation that involved Sherman Watts. And then he'd hushed her, touched her—soothed her fears and anger and her constant fight to be strong and independent—and the years between them melted away. She'd wanted nothing more than to burrow against his big chest and feel his sturdy arms around her again. She'd wanted the shelter he offered as much as she'd wanted to welcome his kiss.

Felt a hell of a lot like *need* to her.

"No." The wall beside her reacted to her firm insistence about as well as her turbulent emotions did. "It couldn't work then. It won't work now."

There. Better. Think it through.

She was leaving tomorrow, Sunday at the latest, depending on how well Watts cooperated with her. She was too smart to risk her heart on a relationship that couldn't last. Ethan was a man of the earth; she was a woman of the city. He was a Bia, son of a successful business owner and a tribal elder, a well-respected name on the reservation. She was a Kuchu, reservation trash, daughter of Ralph, a charmer with a big heart whose addictions had cost him his money as soon as he'd earned it, and Naomi, a flirtatious beauty whose drunk driving had gotten them both killed.

Joanna was too fractured inside to believe in anything more than what she could do for herself and control with her own two hands. What she *needed* was to keep moving forward with her life.

A mystic force of nature like Ethan Bia didn't fit into her plans. She stood a better chance of surviving this trip home if he wasn't a part of it.

"So get over it, already." Smoothing her expression and her thoughts into business mode, she found Patrick Martinez pacing a rut into the carpeting of his office.

"Are you kidding me? Hell." He cursed into his cell phone as he peered outside his window into the waning daylight.

Joanna's training buzzed her senses on alert. What was he looking for? "Sheriff Martinez?"

"Yes. Lock it down before this rain gets worse and washes away any trail he might have left behind. No one goes in or out until I get there." He snapped the phone shut and strode from the office. "Elizabeth!"

"I'm right here, Patrick." The Indian woman set down the two mugs of coffee she carried and took a position at her desk, ready to handle whatever the sheriff needed.

"Sorry." He offered the gruff apology in the same breath he started giving orders. "Get Miguel down from the lab and tell him to scrounge up any of his field techs he can call on short notice. I need them over at Watts's place on the rez ASAP."

"Got it." Elizabeth spared Joanna a quick concerned look at the mention of the suspect's name before picking up the phone and punching in the lab's extension, quickly relaying the sheriff's orders.

"Has something happened?" Joanna asked. Nobody— not Ethan, not Elizabeth Reddawn—had to protect her from Sherman Watts anymore.

Martinez grabbed his Stetson, pointing it at Elizabeth before putting it on. "And call my wife. Tell her I'm going to miss that movie."

Elizabeth nodded, reading off an address she'd brought up on her computer screen.

"Trouble?"

Joanna jumped inside her skin at the sound of Ethan's deep voice from right behind her. How could such a big man move without making a noise?

Martinez nodded to him over her shoulder. "Good. I'm gonna need you with me, big guy."

"Sheriff." Joanna ignored her erratic pulse and insisted on an explanation.

"You might as well come, too, Rhodes. Watts isn't at his trailer. The rat must have gotten wind we wanted to talk to him and skipped town. He's cleared out his stuff and gone to ground." His blue eyes shifted back up to Ethan. "I need you to track him for me."

"My gear's in my truck." A hand at the small of her back guided Joanna into step behind the sheriff as they headed for the exit. "You think we had another info leak?" Ethan asked.

"Who knows?" Martinez paused just inside the doorway. "He probably knows that once we bring him in and he starts talking about Julie Grainger's murder, he won't be going back home for twenty years or so. Maybe his survival instincts kicked in."

Joanna took an extra step to move beyond the distracting brush of Ethan's hand. "You don't believe that."

"No. But I like the idea of having a mole on my team even less than I like the idea of Watts's dumb luck keeping him one step ahead of us." The sheriff pulled his hat low on his forehead before pushing open the door. "Makes me think he doesn't want to answer your questions."

Ethan's growly protest didn't matter. The rain hitting her face didn't matter. Joanna hurried out to the Suburban she'd arrived in, purposely choosing the sheriff's ride over Ethan's pickup.

"He'll answer them," she vowed.

Her ability to leave Mesa Ridge once and for all, knowing Sherman Watts and her past no longer had any hold over her, depended on it.

Chapter Three

Ethan knelt at the edge of the road to study the two smears of black rubber marking the bump where Sherman Watts's yard met the asphalt. A quick analysis of the tread pattern in the mud matched the new, all-terrain tires Watts had been sporting on his beat-up black truck the past couple of weeks. Their suspect had been gone for several hours now.

But Ethan's thoughts had drifted back several years.

"So how do you know it's a buck that left these tracks?" Joanna asked, her knees down in the dirt on Ute Mountain, right beside his. "And not a doe or even a mountain sheep or elk?"

"The size of the print tells me it's a deer. The depth of the depression tells me it's a heavier animal—bigger than a doe or fawn." Ethan pushed aside her raven-colored ponytail that the wind had tangled and the pine needles from where they had left their earthy scent when they'd stopped for lunch and a rest. He fought off the urge to bury his face in the fragrant silk, and continued the lesson. He reached around her, bringing her back nearly flush against his chest as he pointed to the

rounder, softer print in the fine gravel beside the deer tracks. "Can you identify that one?"

"Is it a mountain lion?"

"Yeah."

Joanna Kuchu was more than a bright, eager student who took to his lessons about nature the way a parched horse took to water. She was the first girl he'd met who seemed to genuinely enjoy the solitude of a day in the wilderness as much as he did. The adorable ass butting against his thigh as she studied the tracks he'd pointed out had a lot to do with the hormones that seemed to rage out of control every time the two of them were alone together like this.

She turned to face him. "He's tracking the deer, isn't he? That deer is going to be lunch."

Her crestfallen expression demanded some kind of comfort. "Relax, Nüa-rü." The wind whipped a loose strand of hair across her cheek. Ethan brushed it aside and tucked it behind her ear. "The deer will be all right."

Her tongue darted out to moisten her lips, and Ethan's twenty-one-year-old body lurched with anticipation at the innocent gesture. "How do you know?" she asked.

"The lion's prints are older. He came by here two, three days before the deer."

A smile slowly blossomed across her lips, and Ethan couldn't resist. He dipped his head and pressed his mouth to hers, simply warming hers with the touch of his for a moment, allowing her to either accept or reject his desire for something more.

When her hand settled on his chest and her lips pushed against his, he licked the seam of her mouth, tasting salt and shyness and wonder. With a heavy sigh, *her lips parted. Ethan thrust his tongue between them and Frenched her. She laughed against his mouth, played the same teasing trick on him. Soon, she wound her fingers into the long fall of hair at his shoulder and pulled him a little closer, inviting him to deepen the kiss.*

It didn't take him long to be ready for more—for all—of her. His jeans were already tight at the prospect of being with her. But they'd just started these kissing lessons a few days ago and he didn't want to rush her. He wanted Joanna to be as ready and eager for him as he was for her. He just had to be patient. His time with Joanna would come one day, sooner or later. He could be a man and wait.

Maybe sensing the carnal turn of his thoughts, Joanna dropped her chin and ended the kiss. Her lips were pink, swollen, yet still smiling. She trailed her fingers down through his hair as she pulled away. "You can tell all that by looking at the prints?"

"I can tell a lot just by taking my time to look and listen to what's important."

Squinting against the steady drumbeat of rain, Ethan looked up into the blank sky. The low canopy of clouds was bringing night on early. The flashes of lightning in the distant squall line indicated it was only going to get worse.

Bad enough to drive an average man indoors. Bad enough that a skilled outdoorsman like Sherman Watts could use it to mask his escape.

But Watts had never had Ethan Bia on his trail.

As an army ranger, he'd recovered casualities under gunfire in the mountains of Afghanistan. As a search-and-rescue team leader, he'd tracked down a deaf boy who'd gotten separated from the rest of his troop on a winter camping trip here in Colorado, and had led countless other lost, injured or stranded hikers to safety. He'd spent half his childhood and teen years hiking the desert hills and arroyos and the peaks of the Ute Mountains that dominated the southern horizon.

Rain or shine, he could damn well find the fugitive witness Joanna was so desperate to face. Watts had gotten away with rape fifteen years ago. Whatever crimes he was guilty of now, he wouldn't get away again.

Ethan glanced up and down the road, tuning out past and present conversations as federal agents, the sheriff's department and crime-scene investigators worked the scene around him. He listened to the sounds of the earth, smelled whatever scents hadn't yet been washed from the air. Somewhere there was a disturbance that could give him an indication of their fugitive's flight path. Birds taking wing. The odor of fresh oil. The hum of new tires on the pavement. He listened to his intuition, sorted through the knowledge in his head. He nodded as a possible scenario for Watts's escape route formed.

Of course, Martinez and the others would expect a few facts to back up what his instincts were already telling him.

The tire tracks led from just outside the trailer's front door all the way to the black marks on the road. Though the rain was already beating the pattern down into the mud and distorting it, the tread marks could still give him some information. He dipped his first two fingers into the pool of water gathering there, until he touched the gravelly muck at the bottom. Only up to his middle knuckles—a sign that Watts had been traveling fast and light to leave such a shallow impression.

"Hey, you. Hold this."

"I beg your—"

"Right here."

Ethan glanced across the yard at the sharp order from Miguel Acevedo. The evidence technician grabbed Joanna and pushed an umbrella into her hands. She stiffened up like a possum caught in the headlights the instant he snagged her wrist. Ethan pushed to his feet, every muscle in him tensed to…rescue her? Sheesh. From what? A good friend who was simply conveying a sense of urgency? There was no slight, no danger there. Still, he didn't exhale the tension until she relaxed against Miguel's grip and let him pull her into position beside him.

"Just like that," Miguel coached, squatting back down to press a ring mold around whatever he'd found on the ground. "I need to preserve this evidence before the rain washes it away."

Joanna stood in place, dutifully holding the umbrella over his work. "It's Agent Rhodes. Or Joanna. I don't answer to 'Hey, you.'"

"Give me the etiquette lesson later and just hold the thing. Please." Miguel pulled a bag of gypsum mix from his kit and started prepping it to cast a mold of the track he'd found in the mud. "Dylan? Patrick? Ben? He's had company."

As Miguel's brother, Ben Parrish and the sheriff gathered around, Ethan decided to head on over to report his findings, as well—and to provide Joanna with some friendly support she hadn't asked for, probably didn't need and certainly wouldn't admit she might want.

"What do you have?" Patrick asked.

Miguel pointed to an odd shoe print inside the plastic ring. "This is too big to be Watts's. And the pattern's unique enough for me to think we've seen this before. I want to compare it to those footprints we took out at Griffin Vaughn's estate during the blizzard we had earlier this year—when we believe Perkins murdered Vincent Del Gardo while he was hiding out there. If they match up, then we can reasonably assume that Perkins is back in the area."

Ben nodded. "And that Watts is working with him."

"These prints don't tell you that." Joanna's shoulders squared off even straighter at the scoffs and shaking heads from the men in the cirle with her.

"I'd bet my next paycheck this belongs to Perkins," Miguel groused. "See the unusual pattern of the sole? It's from a pair of pricey designer hikers. They're not standard-issue oxfords or the cowboy boots most guys around here favor."

"I'm not saying it's *not* Perkins's print," she argued. "I'm saying the two men aren't together. At least, they weren't when they left."

Ethan opened his mouth to explain the task force's theory about Watts working as a front man for Perkins and the mob, but there was no need to speak.

This newer, more mature Joanna was perfectly capable of defending her own point of view. "If Boyd Perkins *was* prowling around here, he never got inside the trailer. He might not even know that Watts has disappeared."

"How do you figure?" Martinez asked.

"There's no mud inside. Whoever belongs to these shoes was here after Watts left." Joanna pointed to the tire marks Ethan had been checking. "Watts left before the rain started and Perkins got here. There are no other footprints. His truck was the only thing heavy enough to leave an impression in the dirt before it turned to mud. This footprint was left after it started raining."

Brava, Joanna. The corner of Ethan's mouth tightened with the hint of a smile. All those months of tagging along with him and his brother, Kyle, and then just the two of them together, analyzing which animal had left what trail, and how to tell which direction their quarry was heading, had stuck with her.

Patrick nodded. "So we can assume the two men were here at different times. It's possible that we're not the only ones Watts is running from. If Perkins got wind Watts was going to talk…"

No one needed to finish that sentence. They'd all seen what Boyd Perkins was capable of. They had a trail of dead bodies and scarred survivors to prove what could happen when the wrong person crossed his path.

Dylan Acevedo seemed to think Joanna's idea had merit, as well. "So do we still concentrate on Watts? Or use this opportunity to bring in Perkins, instead? If we track one, we're tracking both, right?"

"Let's not get ahead of ourselves," his brother, Miguel, pointed out. "I haven't even proved that this is Perkins's shoe print yet."

"Yeah, but you're ninety-nine percent sure. I can tell, *hermano.*"

Patrick Martinez steered the discussion back into focus. "We concentrate on what we *do* know. I want Sherman Watts in my interview room ASAP. Someone tipped him off about Agent Rhodes and the interrogation, and now he's running. We find him, and he'll lead us to Perkins. And I definitely want to catch him before Perkins can kill my most promising witness." His icy blue eyes slid over to Ethan, looking for answers. "How do we do that?"

Ethan simply nodded, accepting the lead on this particular mission. "What do we know for certain on the timeline?"

Ben answered that one. He nodded to the neat, white trailer across the road. "The neighbor said Watts's pickup was parked out front when he left for work this morning. That was eight hours ago."

"Pretty significant head start," Ethan conceded. But not insurmountable.

Dylan offered his two cents. "I checked his bank account. There were no big withdrawals in the past twenty-four hours. In fact, the guy's practically broke. Though he had upwards of ten grand just a couple of months ago."

"The file says Watts never held a job for more than a few months at a time," Joanna commented. "Sounds like a payoff to me. Unless he's hoarding the cash, what's he spending it on?"

Dylan answered. "New trailer. Tricking out his truck. Jack Daniel's. The casino. He's not hoarding anything."

Ben thumbed over his shoulder toward the trailer. "There's no booze in there, and I've never seen Watts without a flask or bottle. A gun that's registered to him is missing, too. Looks like he's planning to be gone for a while. You got an idea how to run this search, Ethan? This guy doesn't want to be found." He rolled his eyes skyward. "And we all know damn well the rain is working against us."

Pulling back the front of his jacket, Ethan propped his hands at his hips. He wasn't dressed or armed the way he suspected he'd need to be for this pursuit, but his brain was already on the hunt. "We'll have to wait until daybreak to track him. This storm will get worse before it gets better."

Patrick swore. "He'll be in the wind by then. We don't even know what direction he headed." He narrowed his eyes, reading Ethan's expression more carefully. "Tell me you've got something, big guy."

Ethan tilted his head toward the blacktop. "He went down the road."

"Wiseass." Patrick shook his head and the others grumbled. "There's a highway intersection a mile from here. Did he head east toward Durango? West into the desert? South to the mountains? Hell, he could be in Denver, catching a flight out of the country already." He pulled his cell phone off his belt and punched in a number. "I'll have Elizabeth check the regional airports."

Joanna's dark eyes narrowed in reprimand. "This is no time to joke, Ethan."

Who was joking?

She must be out of practice, recognizing the difference between dead serious and his dry sense of humor. But the sheriff could read him better. He lowered his phone. "What?"

Ethan pointed to the north. "He went to see his uncle Elmer at the retirement center in Mesa Ridge. Probably to scam money or maybe a credit card off the old man so that he could buy supplies. He might even be buying a new ride so he's harder to trace."

The fine line of a frown formed between Joanna's

sleek, dark brows. "You got all that from looking at a tire track?"

Perhaps she'd forgotten more than she remembered about life on the rez. No doubt she'd made a point of forgetting. But one of the pleasures—and perils—of Ethan's life was that he never could.

Not the land. Not the war. Not her. Not what had once been so perfect between them. Not the way it had ended. Like her, he could move on. But Ethan could never forget.

"I know the people here—their habits," he explained, as if he were once again teaching her some lesson about nature and life. "Watts left a kitchen full of food, his suitcase and a canteen here. Yet he took his backpack, a bedroll and fishing gear. The man's going into the wild. I can't tell you where exactly yet, but he'll need gas to get there, maybe a different vehicle to mask his trail. Food. Whiskey."

Patrick grinned. "*That's* why we pay you the money. Elmer Watts's nursing home is our next stop. Ben? You and Dylan start running down the local outdoorsman shops and convenience stores. See if anyone has seen our buddy Watts today."

"We're on it."

Ethan turned with Patrick as the two federal agents headed toward Dylan's SUV.

"Wait a minute. What do you need me to do? Here. Thanks." Joanna pushed the umbrella into the hands of a uniformed police officer's hands and circled behind Miguel Acevedo, carefully avoiding any contamination of the shoe print as she hurried to catch up and fall into step between them. "I'm coming with you."

Ethan glanced at Patrick over the top of her head and silently asked the sheriff to give them a minute. Seeing the sheriff move on without her seemed to unsettle her almost as much as the touch of Ethan's hand on her arm. She turned to face him, though if it was out of simple courtesy or a subtle way to evade his touch, he couldn't tell. *Patience,* ta'wa-chi, he reminded himself. This woman had always required patience. "You've already lost a couple of time zones today. You haven't eaten dinner or checked into your hotel room yet. Why don't you let us do the searching and bring Watts to you at the station house? Face him fresh tomorrow."

"I'm not on vacation, Ethan. I'm here to work." She scanned the area around them, then leaned in slightly, dropping her voice to a whisper. "You, more than anybody here, should understand how important it is for me to see this assignment all the way through to the end."

Before or after the rape, he'd never known Joanna to back down once she set her mind on something. Somehow, she must have it in her head that as long as she projected strength, she *was* strong. But unlike the sweet young woman he'd once loved, this mature version of Joanna had forgotten that revealing a vulnerability required far more courage and strength than toughing her way through every difficult situation.

"No one's going to think any less of you if you go back to your room and rest."

"I will."

"Joanna—"

"You can't get rid of me, Ethan. Stop trying."

That she might be covering up or denying those fears and vulnerabilities worried Ethan. He'd seen the strongest of men—one of his best friends from his ranger unit—crash and burn mentally and emotionally on the battlefield after a particularly grueling mission. After that last hellish rescue in Afghanistan, he hadn't been far behind. He'd needed the open space and the quiet of the Four Corners area to find his inner peace again. What did Joanna have that gave her peace? This skinny slip of a woman with the barbed tongue and cool demeanor was priming herself for an emotional meltdown.

"I never once wanted to get rid of you, *Nüa-rü.*" The Ute nickname for the wind, which had become an endearment between them fifteen years ago, slipped out. The word felt right.

But a shiver rippled across Joanna's shoulders before she set them firmly into place. Clearly, it didn't feel right to her. "I imagine Elmer Watts has retired as the reservation sheriff by now. If he's in a nursing home, he can't hurt me anymore. I'm not afraid of him."

"I don't imagine you'd admit to being afraid of anything. But he *can* hurt you." Ethan breathed in the moist air and let it cool his frustration. "Elmer has Alzheimer's. His wife had him committed to the home as his behavior became increasingly erratic and violent, and her health declined. He can be mean."

That tiny frown reappeared between the beads of rain dotting her forehead. "I suppose the staff could tell you if Sherman visited today—or if they saw his truck. I wonder what kind of information we can get from a man with Alzheimer's."

"Are you listening to me? You don't want to see him."

"Sherman Watts is *my* man. I'm going."

"I'm just trying to look out for you." Ethan reached

out to brush away the strand of hair that stuck to her damp cheek, but she blocked his wrist and stopped him before he could touch her face.

What happened next convinced him that this tough-talking ice-princess facade didn't go beyond skin deep. As she pushed his hand down, she altered her grip. She wound her fingers around his thumb and squeezed.

It was the subtlest of gestures. But it was a connection. A plea.

"I don't need looking after, Ethan. I need justice."

Chapter Four

"Now, if you was seventeen, girl, I might be able to look at pressing statutory rape charges. But you're eighteen. Legal age." The salty grit of used-up tears rubbed Joanna's eyes like sandpaper as she blinked the wiry, gray-haired man into focus. Sheriff Elmer Watts rested his hip on the corner of his desk and shifted his chaw of tobacco from one pocket of his cheek to the other. *"I know you've been through a lot this week, losing your mother and daddy both. It's normal to turn to a man—an older man, especially—for comfort at a time like this."*

"Comfort?" Joanna bolted out of her chair. *"He raped me!"*

"So it got a little rough. Doesn't mean you didn't want it. Some women like it that way."

How could any woman...? Gut-deep emotions swirled inside her skull, making her feel light-headed. The stitched-up cut on her left breast, the bruises where she'd been violated, throbbed in protest. The sickening feeling that, no matter how many showers she took, she'd never feel clean again turned in her stomach. How could any woman possibly want any of that?

"You son of a bitch." Joanna slurred her words around the swelling of her split bottom lip.

The sheriff stood, one hand on his gun, the other holding up a reprimanding finger. *"Don't you go cussing me, girl."*

She ignored both warnings and advanced to look him straight in the eye. *"I went to the hospital. They took a rape kit. Do you have any idea how degrading it feels to be touched and probed after…?"* She swallowed the whimper of shame that caught in her throat. No. She would see this through. *"You can't ignore that kind of evidence."*

"I won't hear anything on that for weeks. Alleged crimes here on the rez aren't a priority for the state lab—"

"Alleged?"

"And we don't have the means to process any evidence here. I'm sorry, but that's how it is."

The instant his fingers closed around her shoulders, Joanna yelped and jumped back beyond his reach. *"Don't touch me!"*

The good ol' boy friendliness of his tone vanished. *"You need to get it together, girl, if you want me to take your accusations seriously."*

"Get it together? You aren't going to do anything? Aren't you even going to write any of this down?"

"You're right." He walked around her to open his office door. *"Elizabeth? Will you take this girl's statement?"*

Elizabeth Reddawn stood right outside, no doubt already responding to Joanna's startled cry. The older woman wrapped her arm around Joanna's waist and gently turned her toward the doorway. *"You come on into my office and sit with me, honey."*

The reality of her situation finally registered. Whatever hopefulness had been left inside her after the attack shriveled and died. Joanna paused at the doorway and glanced over her shoulder at the uniformed man. "What about Sherman Watts?"

"I'll look into it. I'll talk to my nephew, I promise."

Elmer Watts wasn't talking now.

Not about anything useful, at any rate.

"When's my wife coming?" Elmer grumbled. "The party starts at seven. She's always running late."

Joanna shifted back and forth behind the wall of men and residential staff in the cramped room. Though she suspected that the width of Ethan's shoulders blocking her view of the retired, white-haired sheriff was no accident, she'd already gotten a glimpse of Elmer Watts. He was a frail, miserable shadow of the man who'd put family before justice fifteen years ago, and had allowed her rapist to escape any kind of prosecution. It was hard not to feel some measure of pity for his infirmities and the blankness behind his sunken eyes. It was harder still not to resent that he could spark any emotion beyond the anger and resentment she'd carried for so many years.

She'd like to blame her edgy mood on her frustration with Elmer's inability to stay focused on Patrick Martinez's questions. She could feel Sherman Watts slipping further and further from their grasp. But she was afraid that the knot in her stomach was due to the fact that, like Elmer, her memories kept slipping back to the past.

"You aren't going to do anything?"

He hadn't given her the answers she needed to hear back then, either.

"Joanie?" Elmer called out. "You'd better get a move on it, woman, or I'll go to the party without you."

The beefy orderly who'd helped Elmer out of bed knelt down beside the septuagenarian's chair. "These men are looking for Sherman, not your wife. She's gone, Elmer. She passed away last year."

"Sherman's gone, too," he insisted. "Ungrateful boy. Where's my wife?"

Patrick pulled his hat up in front of his face and whispered to Ethan, "How the hell is anything that comes out of his mouth going to be reliable?"

"We know that Sherman stopped by before lunch," Ethan reminded him. The orderly who was assisting them had seen Watts's black pickup earlier in the day. He had no idea what Sherman and his uncle had talked about, but a search of Elmer's things showed that his wallet was now missing. Ethan encouraged Patrick to keep asking questions. "Try talking to him sheriff to sheriff."

With a weary sigh that lifted his shoulders, Patrick turned his attention back to Elmer's gaunt features. "I need your help, Sheriff Watts. We're looking for a suspect."

"Put it out on the wire," Elmer answered. "I've only got two cars to patrol this whole reservation. Can't keep up with my own trouble. You'll have to ask the county cops to help."

"I *am* a county cop. We're looking for your nephew, Sherman."

Elmer glanced from man to man to man in the room without answering. He angled his head to peer between Ethan and Patrick. "Who's there? Sneakin' in behind you."

Now he could think and act like a cop?

"He was here earlier." Patrick ignored the old man's

alarm at spotting Joanna and pulled a mug shot photo from his jacket pocket. "Do you remember talking to this man?"

Elmer took hold of the photo. "My wife is coming to the party." He looked over at the orderly and frowned. "Why isn't Joanie here? You need to unlock the doors and let her in."

It was the orderly's turn to shrug as he pushed to his feet and apologized to Patrick. "I'm sorry, sir. He doesn't have a lot of good days anymore. Beyond seeing Sherm's truck leave about noon, I don't know that there's much anyone here can tell you."

Patrick plunked his hat back on his head. "We tried."

Joanna wasn't giving up so easily. She nudged her way between the two men. "Excuse me, Mr....Laughing Horse?" She paused to read the orderly's name tag. "Does Mr. Watts remember incidents and people from his past?"

"Sometimes. It's pretty typical in Alzheimer's patients for more distant memories to stay with them longer than recent ones."

"Good."

"Joanna—"

She ignored Ethan's warning. "He doesn't have to tell us about today. He can help us if he tells us something about the past." She pulled up a stool and sat in front of Elmer's chair. "Do you know who I am?"

Thanks either to Elmer's incompetence or something more purposeful, the chain of evidence on her rape kit had been "compromised." The lack of admissible circumstantial evidence, combined with his recommendation that she was too distraught to make a reliable witness, had convinced the district attorney that there was no point in going forward with charges against Elmer's nephew.

Would he remember how his actions had changed her life? Would he remember the man he'd helped to escape justice once before?

For a moment, his dark eyes narrowed beneath bushy white brows. Then his wizened face creased into a smile that revealed yellowed teeth. Even without the dribble of tobacco juice staining his lips, it wasn't a pleasant smile. "You're the girl who was supposed to marry my nephew. Wound up with that no-good Ralph Kuchu, instead." He sat back in his chair, sneering. "Why are you pestering me, girl?"

Not the way she'd intended this to go. Bile burned at the back of her throat, but she could still make this work. "That was Naomi, my mother. I'm Joanna."

"I can see why you turned Sherman's head." The correction didn't register in his addled mind. His low opinion of her mother, however, was crystal clear. "So when are you and Ralph gonna pay back the money you owe my nephew, you lyin' tramp?"

"Ma'am," the orderly urged. "He can get pretty bitter."

Martinez politely tried to stop her. "Agent Rhodes—"

"Let her work." Ethan's deep voice quieted the room and washed over her misfiring nerves like a soothing hand.

Her nostrils flaring with a steadying breath, Joanna nodded, slipping into the character Elmer Watts could communicate with. "That's right. I'm Naomi. I'm looking for Sherman so I can pay back that money. Have you seen him?"

"You swindled my boy. Promised him things you

never delivered. Did you blow it all at the casino? He loves you, you know."

Sherman Watts's idea of love for her mother had cost Joanna dearly. Far more than the missing two grand that had brought him to her trailer after the funeral that afternoon. Joanna squeezed her hands into fists and continued. "I expect Sherman's pretty mad at me. Do you know where he might have gone? Where he'd go to get away when he's angry or worried?"

"You can leave the money with me."

"No, thanks." Joanna swallowed hard. "I'd like to pay him back personally. Apologize."

"He'd like that." Elmer nodded and shook his head in the same motion. Was his mind wandering away already? "Can't keep that boy at home. If you want to find him, try the Ute Mountains. That boy loves to go fishing."

Mountains. Pretty vague. Pretty vast. About sixty square miles of not enough information. "The Utes are a big place. Anywhere in particular he likes to go?" Joanna asked.

"Rising Sun Creek is his favorite spot."

Ethan whispered behind her, "That's up on Sleeping Ute Mountain." The mountain cluster's highest peak. "Even a fit climber couldn't get that far in five hours."

Joanna absorbed the information without taking her gaze from Elmer. "Where else does he like to fish?"

"McElmo Creek. Across from the bluffs along the Silverton River. It'll be flooded this time of year with the spring runoff pouring into it. He might find a spot on the bluff side, though. Fishing won't be too good with the current that strong, but—" the old man leaned forward, crooking a gnarled finger to invite her to come closer "—I expect fishing isn't what you have in mind." He pulled back, chuckling. "To hear Sherm tell it, the two of you never made it out of the tent the first time he took you up there."

His laughter grated against her ears and clawed its way through her self-defenses. Her mother had spent time with Sherman on the mountain? Willingly? Or had he forced Naomi the same way he'd forced her daughter? Was that why she'd suddenly dropped one man and turned to a big, lazy lug like Ralph Kuchu? Was that why Naomi had turned to alcohol? Why there'd always been such animosity between their families?

The familiar nightmare tried to sneak its way into her brain, but Joanna slammed the door on the painful memories. "So where will I find him this time of year, Elmer? Rising Sun Creek or the Silverton?"

But the conduit of lucid communication was already closing. "Sherm grew up on those mountains. Knows them better than his own room at home."

"You're sure he'd go up Sleeping Ute Mountain?" She could confirm that much, at least.

"Sometimes he'll disappear for days on end, and come back with more fish than his aunt can cook in a week. Then the rivers dry up to a trickle and he turns to hunting rabbit or deer."

Joanna reached out, needing a definitive answer. "Elmer—"

He slapped her hand. "When are you gonna pay what you owe, you whore? You ruined him, I tell ya. Ruined him. Get out of my house, you no-good Kuchu!"

If someone called her name, she didn't hear it. If she let professional protocol slide when she kicked over the stool and shoved her way past Patrick Martinez, she didn't care.

Joanna dashed out the door, hurried down the hallway and shoved open the front door. She didn't stop when the rain splashed in her face. She didn't stop when the cool air hit her lungs. She didn't stop when a bolt of lightning pierced the night and sent a wave of goose bumps pricking over her skin.

The answering thunder drummed along her pulse and kept her moving until the past finally overtook her.

"You owe me, Naomi." Sherman Watts's words slurred together as he backed Joanna against the counter in the kitchen. "I'm never gonna get the money Ralph owes me now. But we can work out some other kind of payment."

"I'm not my mother," Joanna pleaded, turning her face from his sour breath and desperately searching the small trailer for a way she could escape him. "I know I look like her, but I'm Joanna. Naomi's dead. You were at her funeral this afternoon. You've had too much to drink and you're not thinking straight. You're making a mistake."

"My only mistake was letting you get away from me in the first place. I miss you, baby."

And then his grubby fingers touched her hair.

Joanna groaned with the effort it took to block the rest of the memory before it played itself out. At some point she'd stopped running and was clutching a two-fisted grip around a wall of black steel—the tailgate of a black pickup truck in the parking lot. She blinked the rain from her eyes and stared hard at the red imprint of Elmer's hand on her skin.

"Get over it," she coached herself, squeezing her

roiling emotions out through her fingertips into the unbending steel. "Do your job. Just do your job."

But the red mark stung. The rain trickled along her scalp, cooling her skin to match the chill within. Naomi Kuchu hadn't been a great mother, but Elmer Watts had no right to call her names. No right to strike—

"You okay?"

Joanna jumped at the deep voice behind her. Ethan. She jerked her head in a nod as he moved in beside her.

"The death grip on my truck makes me think…" His big hand covered both of hers, short-circuiting the chaos inside her. "Damn. You're ice-cold, *Nüa-rü*."

"Don't call me that." She pulled her hands from beneath his, swiped the rain from her eyes and retreated from the broad chest and moving arms and concern. "I'm fine."

"I've known you to be headstrong and independent. But you never were a liar."

"I'm not…" His dark brown jacket swirled around her shoulders, interrupting her protest. She immediately tried to shrug it off, but Ethan pulled the collar together at her neck. She shoved at the placket. "Please. I don't need—"

"Stop. Just stop." His knuckles brushed the underside of her chin as his grip on the jacket easily outmuscled hers. As soft as the caress of his voice, the action stilled her.

Joanna tilted her chin and looked up into his eyes. The pools of midnight-brown said he knew where Elmer's words had taken her. The weight of secrets heaved inside her chest and eased out on a long sigh.

She was soaked to the skin, but she was warm.

She was blind with pain and anger and fear, but she could see a light of hope, a shelter to move toward, inside those irises of pure dark brown. "Ethan, I shouldn't—"

"Shh." He stroked his fingers lightly beneath her chin again. Nerve endings awakened, remembered, beneath the comforting touch.

A woman could lose herself in the depth of those eyes. When she was eighteen years old, she'd found understanding there. Caring. A faith in her that she'd longed for, but in the end, couldn't believe.

There were lines etched beside those eyes now, a few as deep and craggy as the rugged landscape he loved so well. There were secrets hidden there, too— secrets the young Ethan had never kept. The Ethan standing before her now, taming her with his gentle touch and deep, hushed voice, was a seasoned, more potent version of the young man she'd loved. He was a bigger mystery to her now than he had ever been. The years had taken the faith from his expression, but the caring was still there.

It was a caring she didn't deserve. And yet... A yearning for something lost, something new to be discovered, sprouted like a tiny seed inside her, waiting to be nourished. Infused with his scent and warmth, Ethan's jacket reminded her of what it was like to be sheltered and claimed by this man. She inhaled a deep, stuttering breath and pushed her hand through the front opening so that she could reach up and touch the sharp angle of his cheekbone.

He wore his Ute heritage beautifully, proudly. Far better than she or her parents ever had.

"You're getting wet." She brushed the rain from the smooth leather of his skin, savoring the friction beneath her fingertips.

"So are you." The corner of his mouth crooked into a smile, luring her touch to the spot.

A slow breath warmed her fingers as his lips parted. A different warmth, deeper inside, unfurled as he pressed a kiss to a lucky fingertip. She remembered his mouth, maddeningly patient, excruciatingly thorough, pressed against her own as he'd taught her what passion between a man and woman could be—should be.

Lightning flashed in the sky overhead, reflecting heat in the night of his eyes, sparking the desire to bring the best part of her past to life again. Her own lips parted as she stroked her finger across the firm male line that ended with a tiny scar at the opposite corner. Like the closely cropped style of his raven's-wing hair, the scar was new.

There was a lot to admire in the changes she was discovering in the mature man. Plenty of ridges and hollows of muscle being revealed as the rain plastered his white dress shirt to his skin. Plenty of raw, masculine energy in the sheer size of him. Parts of her body strained to move closer to his earthy scent and heat. Even the physical battery and scars of her rape hadn't dimmed the memory of how intoxicating a kiss from Ethan could be. Though she'd dated a few men in recent years, she'd struggled with intimacy. Even before the rape, it had been hard to trust or depend on anyone besides herself. Her parents had always depended on her, not the other way around. After their deaths, after the rape and the debacle of justice that followed, it had just been easier, safer, to concentrate on her career because it required an emotional detachment that kept her sane, kept her functioning—allowed her to succeed. But her choices also kept her lonely.

Could Ethan sense the attraction he rekindled inside her? Could he also sense the reluctance to act on the need that simmered in her veins?

Of course he could. What few details Ethan's eyes missed he seemed to intuit with that sixth sense of his. Joanna curled her fingers into her palm and offered a rueful laugh. "Seems I don't have my act together any better than I did fifteen years ago, does it?"

"You've got nothing to apologize for." He tucked his fingers beneath the collar of his jacket, closing it more securely around across her chest. "All those years you took care of your parents, putting them first. And now it seems as though you put your job first. When are you going to start taking care of yourself?"

"I am. I just…" She wound her fingers around the nubby tweed of his lapels, denying the urge to reach out to the man himself. "I didn't expect Elmer to say things that would take me back to that day. It felt as though, after all this time—after all the work and therapy I've done—that nothing had changed. The Watts family always said I'd asked for what happened to me. I wasn't prepared for that."

Ethan's hands slipped to her shoulders, instilling his warmth with a gentle massage up and down her arms. "Did you want the old bastard to show remorse? Elmer doesn't even remember who you are."

"I know." Joanna shook her head. "I can't let him get to me. Every day I put together profiles on murderers, kidnappers, drug dealers and more. This shouldn't be any different. I talk to people. I get inside their heads. It's what I do. I can't let it be personal."

"It's already personal. You barely survived once—"

"You don't think I can survive this place again?" Joanna tugged the jacket from her shoulders and pushed it into the middle of his chest, forcing him to take hold of it—forcing her fingers to let go and pull away. She didn't need his warmth. She didn't need his caring. She didn't need him to make her feel weak or vulnerable or dependent on anyone again. "I'm not a girl anymore, Ethan. I'm not a victim. I'm going to prove that I can do this."

Her eyes filled with rain, and she had to blink away the moisture before he finally spoke.

"Walk away from this assignment, Jo. Walk away before you can't outrun the demons anymore."

"What do you know about demons? I know you mean well, but you can't possibly understand what I've been through—what I need in order to make my life whole again."

"Demons come in many forms." The deadness in his tone was more unsettling than the words themselves. "Trust me, I know exactly how hard they are to shake."

"What does that mean?" Was there something in that comment that explained the harder edges and protective obsession of this older, more cryptic Ethan Bia? Did he think what had happened to her fifteen years ago was somehow his fault? That the challenges she faced now could be solved by anyone besides herself? He pulled his keys from his pocket and circled around her to the cab of his truck. She turned and followed. "Ethan? Don't speak to me in riddles. Talk to me."

"Agent Rhodes?" Patrick Martinez's voice called from the nursing home's front door.

Joanna huffed at the untimely interruption, and glanced over her shoulder to see the sheriff approaching them across the parking lot. She quickly caught up to Ethan, stopped him by laying a hand at the center of his back. "This is my battle, Ethan. I'll be okay." Her issues were her own to deal with.

"It should have been *our* battle." He spun around, leaning in close enough that his chest pushed against her hand before she could snatch it away. "Is it because I didn't protect you from Sherman Watts?"

What? "You couldn't know—"

"Is that why you didn't give me a chance to help you afterward? You didn't believe I'd be there for you?"

"I had to find my own strength. I couldn't do that here. And you couldn't leave. You belong here. I wasn't about to turn your life upside down in an effort to save mine."

"You never even asked. We could have talked about it."

"I was eighteen and damaged and scared out of my mind. I didn't know how."

That fathomless gaze captured Joanna for a moment, reached down to her, found its way beneath her defensive armor, conveying emotions as deep and turbulent as her own. Then, as abruptly as he'd breached her personal space, he retreated. "You have to tell Patrick."

"Tell me what?"

Ethan was hurting. He was angry. She seemed to have a bad habit of bringing out those negative feelings in him. Guilt warred with the feminine instinct to wrap him in her arms and get him to share his secrets. To listen and comfort the way he had with her just a moment ago. She owed him so much more than the few minutes she could give him before climbing onto a plane and leaving Kenner County again as soon as her interview with Watts was completed.

Because that was how this reunion was destined to play

out. She hadn't come back to resurrect a relationship with Ethan. She would never drag him into her world again. She'd never allow her world to hurt him again.

So she pasted on a smile and turned to face Patrick. "I guess we're climbing a mountain."

"*I'm* climbing the mountain," Ethan corrected, casting a shadow like Sleeping Ute itself as he stepped up beside her. "You can do the talking once I bring Watts in."

"Good work in there," Martinez complimented her. "Sorry it got ugly, but that intel definitely narrows our search." Patrick pulled his hat forward to shield his eyes as he looked up into the storm clouds overhead. "Provided we can get anywhere tonight. The chopper will be useless until this clears. As long as there's lightning, I won't allow a search team to take it up."

An expressionless mask slid into place on Ethan's face before Joanna could get a clear read on what he was thinking. "We can catch him on foot. I know the paths he'd most likely take, and have a couple more ideas on fishing holes he might go to. But we'll need daylight. The rocks will be treacherous enough with all this rain. Elmer was right about the rivers and creeks topping their banks. And washouts on the trails are pretty common since the rest of the year is so dry."

Patrick shifted his gaze to Joanna. "I suppose the FBI will want to take over the pursuit?"

Ethan shook his head, denying her the chance to answer. "It's too dangerous for inexperienced climbers to tackle the ascent under these conditions."

"I'm not an inexperienced climber," she argued. "I grew up with those same mountains."

"The terrain can change a lot in fifteen years."

"You'll need as many eyes as you can get to help with the search."

"Whoa. Am I missing something?" Patrick raised his hands, signaling a time-out as Ethan's will to take care of her warred with Joanna's need to take care of herself.

Joanna curled her lip between her teeth. Arguing in front of the ranking local officer wouldn't earn her any cooperation, or a good review for her boss back in D.C. "No, sir. Ethan and I just…see the way to proceed differently."

There was no mistaking where Martinez chose to put his trust. "Ethan's been running search and rescue for Kenner County for the past three years. When it comes to finding someone on those mountains, it's his call."

Ethan's call was equally clear. "I'll take in a small team who know what they're doing. If the FBI is joining the search, they'll be under my command."

"I'll tell them," Patrick agreed. "Safety first."

"I'll round up a couple more guides—men who've worked S and R with me know the area. We'll assemble at the north trailhead of Sleeping Ute Mountain at daybreak. We can each take a destination and pray the weather hasn't washed away every trace of Watts's path. If we travel light and move fast, we should be able to close ground on him." Ethan's tone held none of the warmth he'd shown Joanna a few moments earlier. "I don't want anyone on that mountain who doesn't know what he's doing. My best men will be tied up with the search. Communication may be spotty, and if I have to spare them for a rescue, we could lose Watts."

The sheriff gave a wry laugh. "You have any *good* news for me?"

"Watts is dealing with the same weather and hazards. That should slow him down. He won't make it to Rising Sun Creek tonight. He'll have to make camp somewhere along the way. Even if he moves on in the morning, finding his camp will put us on a clear trail."

"Get your men lined up," Patrick ordered. "I'll get on the horn to Ben and Dylan. I expect Tom Ryan will want to be part of the search, too." He grumbled as he pulled his phone from his belt. "I hate calling a man in from his honeymoon. Agent Rhodes, can I give you a lift to your hotel?"

She wanted to stay with Ethan and find out what miracle he had up his sleeve to track down Watts. She wanted to be on that hike tomorrow morning and be a part of bringing Watts in herself. As difficult as it would be to face her rapist across an interview table, it would be impossible to find closure and move on with her life if Watts disappeared into the wilderness and she never even got the chance to nail him for his more recent crimes.

She had to make Ethan understand that.

But he was already climbing into his truck. The conversation was over.

"Yes, Sheriff, thanks. I'll be right there." Joanna hurried to the truck cab and caught the door before Ethan could close it. "Ethan?"

He peered through the windshield, straight ahead into the night.

But Joanna had made a career out of getting people to talk. And sometimes, that meant she was the one who had to open up first. Inhaling a steadying breath, she stepped into the Vee formed by the truck frame and door. "I'm sorry I hurt you. That was never my intention. You were the best part of my life here."

"Yeah. Things were so good between us, you had to leave." Sarcasm was a new twist to Ethan's personality. But he was talking.

"I had to survive." Tears burned in the corner of her eyes, but she blinked them away. She had to keep the emotion out of her voice and say exactly what she needed to. "I would have gone nuts if I'd stayed here. People on the rez and in Kenner City already talked about me—talked down to me—because of Mom and Dad. They were either going to pity me or laugh at me because I was stupid enough, helpless enough, naive enough—whatever—to let the Watts men take advantage of me. I couldn't handle all that and heal. My problems would have destroyed us. I would have brought you down with me. You couldn't fix me or the situation. No one could. I had to get away. I'm a stronger woman now. Like you said before, it was the first time I ever put myself first. I left because that's what *I* needed. I'm just sorry you had to pay the price."

Apparently, her explanation was fifteen years too late. For the longest time, he just sat there, staring into the rain, saying nothing.

"Ethan?"

"So facing the worst part of your past—entirely on your own—and beating it, is the ultimate therapy for you?"

"Something like that." Lightning flashed overhead, and the answering thunder urged Joanna a step closer. She lightly brushed his pant leg, asking him to listen a little bit longer. "Can you really find Watts after a night like this?"

Not entirely on her own.

Ethan glanced down at her hand, then turned in his

seat, slowly assessing, then accepting her unspoken request. "I'll bring him in if that's what you need from me."

She summoned a shaky smile. "That's what I need."

He reached out, palmed the back of her head and pulled her up onto her toes as he bent his head to cover her mouth in a deep, hard kiss. Joanna's fingers dug into his corded thigh. Her lips parted in surprise, then welcome. His tongue snuck inside to dance with hers and she moaned at the raspy caress that tasted of earthiness and man. She braced a hand against the damp wall of his chest, leaned in. Kissed him back.

Ethan's hand found its way to the curve of her hip and her feet left the ground entirely as he lifted her into the heat and hardness of his upper body. The rain splashed a cool warning against her cheeks, but Joanna ignored it. She wound an arm around his neck, found an erotic stubble of short hair at his nape to rub her palm against instead of the silky, shoulder-length strands where she'd once tunneled her fingers.

It was a kiss of rediscovery—of years gone by and apologies accepted. It hinted at life lived and changes made and opportunities missed. This kiss was more seasoned and sure than the ones she remembered. There was no youthful exuberance, no hesitant testing the waters. It was a grown man's kiss of passion. A kiss of promise.

Joanna was breathless and hot by the time he pulled away.

She sank back onto her heels, her fingers still hanging on to his wet shirtfront, his hands still clamped possessively at her neck and hip. She'd felt no fear of Ethan when he kissed her. But Joanna feared what his kiss made her feel. "I—"

"Don't say anything." Ethan's dark eyes glowed like obsidian glass in the light from his truck. "I've missed you so much, *Nüa-rü*. I've needed you. I remember when you were all sunshine and curiosity and a strong, forgiving heart. I needed that."

She frowned with confusion, ached with compassion, at the sorrow heard in his voice. "Ethan—"

"Shh." He pressed a finger to her lips. "I'll do this for you. I may not understand it, but I'll do whatever it takes to get the spirit Watts stole from you back." His uneven breath fanned warmly across her cheek as he rested his forehead against hers and made her a promise. "Watts may know those mountains. But I know them better."

Chapter Five

"Love to love ya, baby…"

Sherman Watts sang a familiar melody, his eyes closed, his hand stroking his thigh from crotch to knee, remembering better times up here on the mountain. The air crackled with electricity from the storm. His clothes were wet and sticking to his skin. But ghostly memories blended with reality. He didn't care about any discomfort he should be feeling.

The chilling mist that dotted his face blended with visions of long black hair, sweetly perfumed, caressing him. The thunder added percussion to the music playing in his head. He pursed his lips around the mouth of his Jack Daniel's bottle and tipped it back, letting the whiskey ignite a fire all the way down to his belly.

He licked the rim of the bottle, stroked his thigh and pretended he wasn't alone. "I need your—"

The shrill chirp of a cell phone startled him from his hazy fantasy. Sitting bolt upright, he knocked the bottle from his lap. "Son of a bitch."

A pool of amber liquid sank into the dust. Cursing at the waste, and his ungainly movements that couldn't right the bottle faster, he stopped to pound the cork into the bottle before he reached into his pack to grab the phone. He leaned back against the back wall of the shallow cave where he'd taken shelter and flipped open the phone. There was only one caller who ever contacted him on this line.

"What do you want?"

"Boyd Perkins is looking for you."

Sherman wasn't so far gone with lust or drink that his head couldn't clear fast. He braced his hand against the gritty sandstone wall and staggered to his feet. For a moment the rustle of static in his ear made him wonder if he'd heard right. "Boyd Perkins?"

"Yeah. He's got a job for you."

"Now?" He turned his mouth to the phone, raising his voice over the noise of the thunderstorm that was draining the sky. "You told me to disappear. That's what I've done."

"The sheriff and that hotshot agent from D.C. talked to your uncle this evening." His caller paused. "They plan to launch a search up in the mountains tomorrow morning."

That news deserved a curse. Or two. But he'd discovered places in these mountains that his dear old uncle never knew about. "Thanks for the heads-up."

But he wasn't that worried. The feds would still be chasing shadows long after he made his way down the far side of the range and was miles away from Kenner City. It was his plans for surviving *after* he left the mountains that needed a little fine-tuning, especially when he hoped his work for Perkins would give him an inside track on getting some jobs in Vegas. Failing to be at Perkins's beck and call now could mess up his plans for later.

He hated that he was even tempted to ask, "What exactly does Perkins want?"

Was that laughter he heard through the static? "They just pay me to be the messenger. You'll have to work the details out with him."

"How am I supposed to do that? I can hardly meet him at my place. You know the cops are watching it." The measly fire he'd built was giving off more smoke than heat because everything around here was so freaking wet. Including him. He looked past the smoky embers into the darkness beyond the lip of the cave. He needed to be sharp to make sense of the shadows and night surrounding his perch here on the bluffs of the Silverton River. If he couldn't distinguish a rock or a tree from a man, he could end up caught.

Or dead.

Storm or distance or both garbled his contact's reply. "All he said was…family loyalty… The feds have a decent lead on your whereabouts, and Perkins insisted…can use you. And then he'll help you get out of the country."

Sherman's attention shifted as he slipped and kicked a rock into the smoky fire. The hiss of damp wood tumbling closer to the heat was an uncomfortable reminder of the danger of his situation.

Wait a minute, Sherm. Think.

"You son of a bitch." That's what this phone call was really about. His contact thought he could outsmart ol' Sherman.

No. Way.

"Am *I* the job? What did you say to him? He knows I'll keep my mouth shut. Nobody's gotten a word out of me for six months. Did Perkins put you up to this?" The cell phone might hold a secure number, but anyone who knew it could put the code into the system if he had access to the technology required to locate pings on cell towers. And this guy had access, he was certain of it. Though he didn't have a name—his instructions had always come over the phone or through Perkins himself—his contact knew too much about the KCCU and the FBI's investigation to be anything but an inside man.

"Don't get your shorts in a knot. He said...lead on Del Gardo's money. If you distract the agents and deputies looking for you while he...meet up...Vegas and then get you out of the country."

"What?" he shouted through the static.

"Perkins...your help...pay well." More static.

"Are you tracing this call? Reporting my location to him?" Why would a cold-blooded hit man bother with pulling him out of hiding for one more job? Why would he go to the effort of sneaking him out of the country when he could lure him to a meeting with the promise of money, then silence him permanently with a bullet or a garrote? A job right now didn't make sense.

This bozo didn't make sense. "Sherman—"

"To hell with you. And to hell with the money."

He disconnected the call. Turned off the phone. He went to the cliff's edge and hurled his last link to civilization into the chasm below.

He swatted the water off the brim of his hat and plunked it on top of his head. So much for his trip down memory lane and a few hours of sleep. He kicked the biggest logs from the fire, scattering them out into the rain to douse the flames and smoke. Hell. Why not just send up a signal flare? Come morning, even a tenderfoot could spot where his fire had been. The roar and splash of the swollen river crashing over the rocks below him gave him an idea.

Kneeling beside his pack, he pulled on the work gloves he'd bought and picked up the glowing logs. Following the sounds of the river, he inched his way to the edge of the bluff and tossed the remains of his fire into the water. He never heard, much less saw the evidence of his camp get swallowed up by the depth and fury of the river racing through the darkness below.

Sherman had lived without money before.

He could *live* without it again.

With the rain promising to pour down around him throughout the night, he opened his pack and pulled out a small shovel and went to work. He could spare thirty minutes or so to ensure that anyone who *was* lucky enough to spot this location—be it cop or hit man— would be slowed down and hopefully thrown off course.

Then he turned up the mountain, making a path of his own and erasing it behind him as he disappeared into the night.

RED AND ROSE AND orange chased away the gray gloom of the rainy night as dawn colored the rugged landscape.

Joanna tilted her face to the eastern horizon, trying to soak in those first rays of sunlight amid the efficient bustle and clipped conversations of setting up a command post at the base of the Ute Mountains. *"I remember when you were all sunshine and curiosity and a strong, forgiving heart."* Ethan's words after that emotional armor-dissolving kiss last night had hinted at new wounds inside him, something he needed that her absence—her abandonment—had denied him. Had she changed so much? Held her heart in rigid stasis for so long that she no longer had the power to give to someone she cared about?

And she did care about Ethan. She'd allowed the love she once felt to grow dormant. But they'd been through too much together—reservation gossip about that poor, disreputable Kuchu girl dating the tribal elder's son, escaping the demands and embarrassment of her parents, losing them—for Ethan not to hold a special, honored place in her life.

She missed feeling passion for something more than her job. She missed how normal it felt to be held in a man's arms and want him desperately. He'd given her a taste of both last night. She hadn't seen the full sun in almost thirty-six hours and wanted to embrace its heat. She wanted to be able to embrace life—and relationships, as well—the way she once had.

But she was going back to Washington, D.C. when this case was over. Getting involved with Ethan and leaving him was a cruelty she didn't intend to inflict on him twice. The whole idea of hurting that good man again made her shiver. In spite of her turtleneck and an insulated down vest over her jeans and boots, the sun couldn't warm her on the outside, and her good intentions didn't offer much warmth from the inside, either.

"Look at it while you can." She startled as the young man who'd introduced himself as Bart Flemming reached past her into the back of the SUV where she stood. "We're supposed to have another storm by later today. All this rain makes it damn hard to work on my tan."

Though he'd misread her introspective shiver and her

fascination with the sunrise, Joanna laughed as she was meant to. But Bart's joke made it easier to switch her focus back to the investigation. In the back of her mind, she tried to calculate just how many hours of daylight and clear sky they'd have before the next wave of severe weather forced them to turn back from their search for Watts. "You think it'll hold off until this evening?"

"It better." Bart picked up a portable generator for the tent where the crime unit, FBI and sheriff's department were setting up their base camp at the edge of the gravel parking lot. "You want to grab those cords and my laptop?"

"Sure. Is that everything?"

"Yeah. Go ahead and close it up." Bart, whose spiky brown hair stuck out in a half dozen directions, was the self-described techno wizard of the KCCU lab. According to his animated conversation all the way from downtown Kenner City, his job this morning was to rig up a complex system of radio, satellite and online communications at the remote location. Since he'd been kind enough to swing by the hotel to pick her up, she'd volunteered to help him unload his field equipment from the SUV.

Joanna looped the strap of the duffel bag filled with power cords over one shoulder, then picked up the computer case with her free hand. She nudged the SUV shut with her hip and followed him to the open-sided tent.

"Dump the laptop at my station." Bart directed her to one table before disappearing beneath another one. "Then bring the cords over here. I have to get us hooked up to the lab so that Miguel can have them run some prints through AFIS."

She followed the direction of Bart's finger over to the

far side of the lot where Miguel Acevedo from the crime lab was processing a beige-and-rust Chevy pickup cordoned off by official yellow tape. Though Elmer Watts's information had led them to this area, confirming that the fingerprints on the abandoned truck belonged to Sherman would make everybody on the scene feel a lot more confident that they were closing in on his trail. Switching vehicles was not uncommon for a man on the run, but thus far Watts's newer truck hadn't been found. Evidence they could retrieve from this old junker might allow them to retrace Sherman's actions over the past twenty-four hours, including pinpointing any accomplices or even verifying whether or not Boyd Perkins was back in the area.

Knowing where Sherman had gone and who he'd been talking to would benefit her interrogation, as well. Reason enough to quit thinking and start moving.

Hefting the heavy bag higher onto her hip, Joanna wove her way around equipment and personnel, swinging her gaze over to the group of men gathering at the back of Ethan's pickup truck and sharing an animated conversation. He didn't have to stand taller than the others for her to notice him. Ethan Bia wore an air of calm serenity about him that commanded attention. It might be the military training Elizabeth Reddawn had mentioned. Or it might simply be that Ethan Bia was as at home in the rugged outdoors as Bart was in his computer lab.

Ethan's dark gaze slipped across the parking lot to find her staring. He held her eyes for the longest of moments. Then he gave her a slight nod, sharp as a salute yet intimate as a caress, before turning away to answer a question from the man beside him.

Oh, Lord. She was finally feeling that burst of warmth that had eluded her earlier. She pressed her knuckles to her cheek. Definitely blushing.

"Smooth one, Joanna," she chided herself on a whisper. *Real professional.* She wasn't wearing a gun at her hip so that she could reminisce about late-night kisses and racing pulses and promises made between former lovers. She was here to conduct business.

With a flare of her nostrils, she inhaled deeply. As she exhaled, she set aside the purely female thoughts that had snuck into her brain and forced herself to think like an agent. Observe. Assess. Decide. Act.

Besides Sheriff Martinez and the FBI agents she'd met yesterday—Ben Parrish and Dylan Acevedo—she vaguely recognized the two other Native Americans with Ethan. Men from the reservation about her own age, maybe former schoolmates grown up. They probably knew the Four Corners area as well as Ethan. Working with an all-business precision, the Ute men were suiting up with multipocketed hiking vests and light backpacks. The two agents wore similar backpacks, but instead of strapping on ropes and pitons and water bags, they were checking magazine clips on their guns and adjusting holsters beneath the Kevlar vests they wore.

The bag she carried weighed heavily on Joanna's shoulder. She should be suiting up and joining those men. Instead, she'd been relegated to pack-mule duty. Not that she didn't understand or appreciate the importance of prepping and manning a cohesive command center to coordinate search efforts across such a vast area of wilderness. But Sherman Watts was *her* suspect, *her* responsibility. Ending his career as a criminal and finding them a new lead on the Julie Grainger murder was her professional mission.

Ending his career as a free man was her personal mission.

Despite Ethan's vehement vow to track down the bastard for her, Joanna's feet shifted with the need to control her own destiny. To be mistress of her own success.

Or failure.

Her gaze dropped to the scrub trees and new grass greening beyond the edge of the tent. No. Failure wasn't an option for her. She couldn't allow herself to even consider the possibility. Losing Watts, or breaking down when she faced him across that interview table, would mean that the past fifteen years of rebuilding her life had been for nothing.

Sherman Watts had taken her trust in men, her confidence in herself and her faith in the world that afternoon in her parents' trailer. She wouldn't let him take anything else from her.

The idea sprouting at the back of her mind needed a few minutes to grow into a workable plan. She needed to figure out a way to take a more active part in bringing in Watts. In the meantime, she'd do the job assigned to her—haul equipment. Adjusting the cord bag higher on her shoulder, she swung around.

And nearly mowed down a fellow agent.

"Easy." Tom Ryan—the newlywed agent Sheriff Martinez had introduced her to when she first arrived that morning—grabbed her by the shoulders and absorbed the brunt of the collision. "Need a hand?"

"I've got it, thanks." Joanna retreated a step and looked up into his stern countenance. An idea was definitely growing. "Congratulations on your marriage, Agent Ryan."

"Thanks." The hint of a smile appeared. "I think I did all right."

Better than all right, judging by the way Bart Flemming had spoken in such glowing terms of Dr. Callie MacBride-Ryan, the crime lab's chief forensic scientist.

"You could have stayed with your wife, you know." Joanna fixed an appropriately considerate smile on her mouth and made him an offer. "I'd be happy to take your place on the search. I grew up in the area, so I know the mountains fairly well. And nobody around here knows Sherman Watts better than I do."

Let him assume her knowledge of Watts and his behavior all came from research files.

Agent Ryan slipped his backpack over his shoulders. He seemed friendly enough, though his expression remained stern, making it difficult to tell whether his next sentence was a compliment or criticism. "Ben and Dylan said you were a go-getter. I appreciate the offer. But I've been on this case from the beginning, and Julie Grainger was a friend of mine. Callie understands my need to see this thing through to the end. Besides, I believe Watts helped the man who tried to murder my wife escape capture. That makes this assignment personal."

He had no idea how well she understood that remark.

"Allegedly helped, you mean. Do you have any proof that Watts is an accessory to attempted murder?"

He checked the clip of bullets on his Glock 9 mm, and

tucked a pair of spare magazines into the side zip of his pack. "You ever been on a manhunt detail, Rhodes?"

"I've worked on several criminal cases."

"Meeting a perp in a closed room isn't the same as tracking him across open territory. Out here, he has the advantage. The unexpected can happen and he can turn at any moment. Suddenly, *you're* the prey and he's the hunter. You stick to your interview room. I promise not to shoot him until you've had the chance to ask him a few questions."

"Shoot…?" Of course he was kidding. Wasn't he? But he was already past her, striding toward Ethan's truck to meet the rest of the search party.

She hadn't considered that there were others working with the crime unit who might have a personal grudge against Watts because of his dealings with Boyd Perkins and the Wayne crime family. She had to believe that they'd all behave in a strictly professional manner, but what if Watts resisted capture? What if he threatened one of the trackers or agents, and they were forced to fire their weapons? They were all trained to stop an attacker. Stopping sometimes meant killing.

Could she ever put the past behind her if she was denied the chance to stand face-to-face with her rapist?

She had to be a part of the search.

"Yo, Rhodes. You coming with those power cords or not?" Bart's summons from beneath the next table prompted Joanna to move. But even as she crawled beneath the table and helped him link the equipment to the field generators, she never stopped thinking about the best way to get on that mountain.

TEN MINUTES LATER, the sun had cleared the horizon and the entire team on-site—searchers and base personnel alike—had converged at the trail head. Patrick Martinez was finishing up his don't-take-unnecessary-risks-out-there speech. "I'm keeping the choppers grounded unless we have a good fix on Watts's location. I don't want to give him any more of a heads-up as to how close we are than he might already have. That means stealth and speed are key. Watch your backs out there—we know Watts took a gun and ammo from his trailer. We have every reason to believe he's armed and dangerous. Miguel?"

The crime-scene investigator stepped forward with a nod. "The truck in the parking lot was reported stolen last night from the casino in Towaoc. The prints on the wheel are definitely Watts's, so we can add that to the list of crimes we suspect him of. I found smudges on the outside of the vehicle, as well, from someone who was probably wearing gloves. The kicker is I found traces of explosives in the bed of the truck. Now, the truck's owner works for a construction company, so it's entirely possible the trace is related to his job."

Patrick nodded. "But don't discount the fact Watts may have done a little shopping himself. He's proven to be a jack-of-all-trades over the years. Wouldn't surprise me if he knows a thing or two about working with C-4. Wouldn't surprise me if those smudges belong to whoever leaked the info to Watts that we were after him in the first place. Eyes open, men. As badly as we want our suspect, I want all of you back here in one piece by sundown." He ended his speech and turned the briefing over to Ethan. "This is your game now, big guy. I know you'll keep it short and sweet."

Though Joanna stood at the back of the gathering, wedged between Bart Flemming and her guilty conscience, Ethan's eyes sought her out. She didn't need her ability to read people's expressions to know he was sending her a message, silently telling her he'd accomplish this mission for her.

Joanna blinked and looked down at the ground, pretending a rapt interest in a small tuft of grass, fighting for life in the gravelly muck at her feet. She rationalized that it was a smart rather than cowardly maneuver, to keep Ethan's intuitive perception from reading her intentions. The pause in his briefing might indicate that he suspected something, but time and the priorities of the moment didn't allow him the chance to probe for more information.

"Since the Ute Mountains are sacred ground, completely encompassed by the reservation, the land has restricted access. That means there are few roads or trails, so traversing them can be difficult." Joanna peeked up to see that his attention had shifted to the sky. "Overnight temperatures will have turned the rain and dew to frost or even ice at higher elevations, so watch your footing. Even dry lightning can be a danger to climbers, but if another storm hits, you'll need to worry about washouts, mud slides and flash flooding, as well. If you get wet, be on guard against hypothermia."

And those were just the natural hazards they'd have to deal with.

"Check your radios. Cell reception out here is unreliable." He shifted his gaze over to Bart Flemming.

"Bart, I need you to coordinate and triangulate our positions here at the command post. I want hourly check-ins. You don't hear from somebody, I want to know about it ASAP."

"Yes, sir."

"And keep an eye on the Doppler radar. I want to know in advance when we're getting a repeat of last night's storm." He looked to Ben Parrish, who was buckling his radio onto his vest. "Ben, you're with me. We'll follow Cottonwood Wash up to Rising Sun Creek on Ute Peak. Joseph, you and Tom circle around Marble Mountain to Whispering Falls. And, Garan, you take Acevedo here through the pass between Horse Peak and Black Mountain. See if you can get as far as McElmo Creek. Good hunting, men."

The group dispersed, with the majority of them moving back to the command post tent. Tom Ryan and his guide headed south into the scrub pine forest at the base of the mountains, while Dylan Acevedo and his guide headed north toward the Canyons of the Ancients National Monument.

"Give me a sec," Ethan said, telling Ben Parrish to start on without him. With a nod, Ben dropped down into an arroyo and moved toward the slope on the opposite side.

Ethan and Joanna were left alone for a few precious moments. He moved silently over the gravel and mud as he walked off the distance between them. "Will you be okay waiting here?" he asked.

In lieu of lying, Joanna chose not to answer. Instead, she reached out and flicked her finger across the handle of the long hunting knife he'd strapped to his waist. "You're not taking a gun?"

"I had my fill of guns in Afghanistan. I don't like to carry one anymore." In a deceptively casual gesture that conveyed something more, he brushed the callused tip of his index finger across her forehead and tucked a loose strand of hair behind her ear. "You worried about me?"

His tone was tender, his touch even more so.

"Yes." She was quick to catch herself and shake her head. "No." *Not for the reason you think.* "I'm sure you'll be just fine. I mean, the wind or the rocks or that sixth sense of yours will tell you the bad guy's coming before he gets there, right?"

"Hope so."

She drummed up a smile. "You'll know. I never have doubted your skills as a tracker."

"Then what's bugging you?"

Joanna's gaze sank to the zipper on his vest. He'd handcuff her to his truck if he knew what she was planning. "Watts getting away. Losing my chance to confront him."

Could he hear the truth in her voice? Could he sense what she *wasn't* saying?

That same finger tapped her beneath the chin and asked her to look up into those beautiful onyx eyes. "He won't get away."

Joanna nodded. Believed. Longed to trust in those words. But ultimately, she knew it was up to Joanna Rhodes to take care of what Joanna Rhodes needed. She peeked around him to nod toward Agent Parrish's disappearing figure. "You'd better get going."

"Stay put. Stay safe."

Joanna's breathing hitched at the dark husk of Ethan's voice. Protocol wouldn't allow a goodbye kiss, and she suspected that the next time they met in private, he'd be more likely to lecture her than to share any affection. Nonetheless, Joanna craved some kind of personal contact with him, something kinder than the tears and running away that had ended their relationship fifteen years ago.

So she pulled his hand from her chin, wrapped her fingers around his and squeezed.

He turned his big hand to engulf hers and squeezed back.

Hidden from the view of any colleagues who might happen to glance their way, Joanna slid her palm along Ethan's. Sensitive nerves awoke. Her skin warmed. Her pulse raced.

"You're a hard man to get over, Ethan Bia."

He leaned forward, ever so slightly. But he came close enough that she could feel the warmth emanating from his body. So much strength. So much heat. Every cell in Joanna's body leaped with the desire to burrow into that warmth. Her lips parted. Her breasts tingled at the tips.

"You were impossible," he whispered.

And then he pulled away. Backed away. Left her standing there with her mouth agape, her insides quaking with a riot of emotions. After all this time, after all she'd done, did he think he still loved her? She didn't deserve that. She couldn't handle it. She couldn't handle hurting him again.

"I'll come back to you, *Nüa-rü.*"

He turned and climbed over the lip of the arroyo, his long legs quickly eating up the ground as he caught up to Ben Parrish.

When he was finally out of earshot, when she could finally squeeze the inevitable truth past the lump in her throat, she answered him.

"No, you won't."

Chapter Six

"Here." Ethan plucked out of the mud the reedy stalk that had been snapped in two. He handed the sign up to Ben and unsheathed his knife to poke aside the tall grass wedged in the triangle between two granite boulders, so as not to disturb the ground. "And here. He came this way. He's trying to keep to the harder surfaces of the rocks to mask his trail." He brushed his hand across the shady underside of the rock and came away with dewy fingers. "But the rocks were probably slick until the sun hit them, and he slipped every now and then."

"You're sure it's Watts and not some big cat or coyote?" Ben Parrish asked.

"The cat's not going to slip." Pushing to his feet, Ethan pointed to the depression captured in the grass at the foot of a granite boulder. "And the coyotes around here don't wear boots."

"Point taken."

Ethan wiped the dampness of his knife blade off on his pant leg and fastened it back in its leather sheath. He pulled the tube from his water pack free and sucked down a couple of good swallows. He reminded Ben to do the same. Drinking water became even more important as the air thinned at the higher elevation. Nasty headaches or muscle cramps could force them to call off the search before they had their man in custody.

Ben pulled off his slim, wraparound sunglasses and shed his pack to retrieve a bottle of water. "Are we sure this is a legitimate trail? At our last check-in, Bart said Dylan and Garan had followed a dummy trail for almost a mile before it doubled back on them."

Ethan nodded. "Watts had a busy day yesterday. But that print was made last night. A lot later in the day than what Garan reported. From what I know about the man, we're on the most likely path. If he truly wants to disappear, this is the way to reach the most rugged, inaccessible part of the mountains."

"My money's on you, big guy." After taking a drink, Ben climbed out onto a granite outcropping to study the steep grade below them. "How high up are we?"

Climbing straight up instead of zigzagging back and forth would have been a shorter, more direct route to the summit, but with the potentially deadly combination of too much water and typically dry soil, Ethan had opted for the longer, safer route. The chance to reach Rising Sun Creek before Watts had been negated by the danger of landslides or a simple misstep with nowhere to fall but way down.

"Considering the base altitude was sixty-two hundred feet above sea level, and we've been climbing for almost four hours, I'd say we're—"

"Pretty damn high." Ben pulled his cell phone off his belt and punched a few numbers. With a shake of his head, he clipped it back onto his belt and rejoined Ethan. "We're out of range."

"No surprise there." The sun was warm on his back through the layers of thermal and flannel shirts he wore, but the air was cool for a spring day—a sure indicator of the next round of storms heading their way by nightfall. Knowing the roughest part of their trek still lay ahead of them, Ethan breathed in deeply, taking stock of his body. He felt no sense of being winded or fatigued—not that he was prepared to rest until he had Watts in his hands. But he'd been hiking the mountains for decades. Ben here was a city boy, certainly fit, but he couldn't afford to be slowed down by a partner who suddenly passed out from exhaustion. "You need a break?"

"Do you?"

Closing his eyes and turning his face toward the sky, Ethan tried to get a sense of company in the area, how much daylight was left, and how willing he was to return to camp to face Joanna without Watts. He might not understand her plan to get rid of Watts's influence over her life by going one-on-one with him in that interview room, but he understood demons. He understood how badly it could gnaw at a person if salvation from those demons was denied.

Ethan still carried that most awful day of the war with him. The day the carnage was too much. The day his team couldn't recover one living soul. The day his buddy, Sam, had cracked on the battlefield and put his own gun to his head.

He slowly opened his eyes, slowly relaxed the white-knuckled grip of his fists at his sides.

Like Joanna, Ethan had come back home to heal.

But unlike Joanna, he'd always believed that reclaiming the best in his life—her, them—was the only way to truly defeat those demons. Joanna believed she had to embrace the worst.

Maybe there was no way they could both have what they wanted. But Ethan would never let her down again. He'd have to die on this mountain before he'd come back without Sherman Watts.

"Ethan?"

He'd been too quiet for too long. But his decision was made and he damn well wasn't going to try to explain just how certain he was that he was doing the right thing to a man—to a world—that needed facts and science to believe anything.

Pulling the radio from his vest, Ethan turned to face his partner. "I'm going to send Joseph and Tom back to base camp with Dylan and Garan."

Ben's eyes narrowed skeptically. "You're calling off the search?"

"I figure we've got three hours before the rain starts up again, maybe an hour of daylight after that."

"Screw the rain. If we give Watts two nights of a head start, we'll never catch him."

Ethan spelled it out in black-and-white. "I'm not turning back. Either I locate Watts or I make camp for the night and find him tomorrow. We're the only ones who have any chance of reaching him at this point. But if we stay, we'll be trapped up here when the storm hits."

"I'm game."

"It'll be a tough night," Ethan warned him.

"You're that certain we're on Watts's trail?"

"Yes."

Ben put on his sunglasses and grinned. "That's good enough for me."

"You want Watts as badly as I do, don't you?"

Ben nodded without offering a reason why. "Call it in. We're not leaving this mountain."

"WHAT AM I SUPPOSED to do?" Joanna's dark eyes were red and puffy with tears. Her skin was pale, making the fist-size bruises on her cheek and jaw stand out in angry relief.

When Ethan had knocked on her trailer door that night and gotten no response, even though a light was on and her car was parked outside, he'd let himself in to check on her. He'd never seen such devastation of property—or woman—in his life. For a few minutes, he'd been in a bit of shock himself. But then the anger had kicked in, clearing his head.

He'd gotten Joanna dressed. Found a clean towel to stanch the bleeding from the wound across the top of her left breast. He'd wrapped his denim jacket around her shoulders to keep her warm.

And now, after buckling her up inside his truck, he handed her the ice pack for her lip, ran around to climb in behind the wheel and start the engine. The police would meet them at the emergency room in Kenner City.

"Nüa-rü, you gotta talk to me. Who did this to you?"

Silence. Hell. His insides were shriveling up with anger and hurt and helplessness. *"Do you know who attacked you?"*

Finally, a nod.

Double hell. *"Who? After the hospital, we have to talk to the cops."*

"They won't listen to me. I'm a Kuchu. They've seen me too many times to believe—"

"You were bailing out your parents! You were taking care of them!" Too loud. Too harsh. Ah, hell. Somebody punch him for making her shrink against the passenger door like that. "I'm sorry. You weren't the one in trouble with the law. They'll listen."

For the longest time, he thought his outburst had silenced her. He was too big a man to be yelling at a woman like that, even if it was out of frustration, or indignation on her behalf. "Talk to me, Joanna. Tell me what happened. I'll listen."

His knuckles turned white around the steering wheel as she whispered bits and pieces of her nightmarish attack into the darkness of the truck cab.

"He hit me when I fought back. He found a knife in the kitchen drawer and cut me. He held it to my throat while he... And then he..." Her soft sob clawed its way straight into his heart.

Ethan had been raised to be a peaceful man. Had made a point of keeping things gentle and patient with Joanna so he didn't scare her off. But he sensed he could murder a man right about now. "Who—?"

"He thought I was my mother. He called me Naomi— kept saying he needed her. Said Mother owed him. He was making her pay."

Just a few hours after burying her mother? What kind of sick bastard would go after a woman while her grief was still so fresh? Who would be cruel enough to use that grief against her?

"Who was it, Joanna? Tell me, and I'll pound the son of a bitch."

For a moment, she roused herself from her shock. "Your father wouldn't approve of that."

"My father wouldn't approve of what happened to you, either."

"You can't get in trouble with the law. Not for me. I'm not worth you losing your father's respect and jeopardizing your future."

"Don't say that." He reached across the seat to squeeze her hand, but she jerked it into her lap almost as soon as his fingers brushed against hers. Curling his fingers into a fist, he pulled away. Of course, she wouldn't appreciate a man's touch right now. He pressed a little harder on the accelerator to get her to the hospital sooner. She needed someone to take care of her tonight. Even if it couldn't be him. "I love you."

"I know."

"Joanna…" What was he supposed to say? How could he make her believe he would always be here for her? "This doesn't change the way I feel about you."

She drew her legs up into the seat and curled her body into a ball. "It changes how I feel."

"About us?"

"About everything."

"Who the hell did this to you, baby?" Her soft, voiceless sobs triggered a gritty dampness behind his own eyelids. She was so hurt. How could he have allowed the woman he loved to get hurt like this? "Who raped you?"

They raced another mile through the night before she spoke again.

"He was drunk."

He quickly narrowed a short list down to one. The SOB had been drinking at the funeral. He had history with her late parents. "Sherman Watts?"

Ah, hell. As he hit the outskirts of Kenner City, Ethan took a silent vow.

That bastard would never hurt Joanna again.

"Up or down? Ethan!" The sharp, authoritative voice cut into Ethan's thoughts. For a split second, he was on recovery recon in the mountains of Afghanistan, and his lieutenant, Sam Keller, was warning him to start talking about where their unit's point man was taking them. "Up or down?"

Ethan had trudged along for an hour, guided by instinct, haunted by the past. But Ben Parrish's urgent voice dragged him back to the present.

"You okay, man?"

Shutting down those old feelings and snapping his gaze into focus, Ethan made a quick survey of the area. Ben was right to demand guidance. Their steady climb was about to get tricky as he eyed the washout on the trail ahead of them. "I'm okay. Take a breather while I check things out."

They'd reached the Silverton River gorge. The roar of the river slamming through the narrow canyon three stories below them drowned out the ominous cadence of thunder that rumbled in the sky overhead. With the charged ions of dropping barometric pressure pricking the short hair at his nape to attention, Ethan was certain he hadn't miscalculated the time of the storm. But anything in the sky sounded closer and more threatening at this altitude.

He hoisted himself up onto one of the scrub pines that had been tipped at a dangerous angle over their path, testing the strength of the exposed roots clinging to the steep incline to their left. After one good bounce, the roots began to lose their grip on the soil and the tree made a deep, yawning sound as it bent closer to the drop-off on their right. Ethan jumped back to the ground, shaking his head.

"Soil's too wet. We can't count on them to hold our weight if you miss a step."

"So I won't miss a step." Ben's sunglasses were long gone, but the keen, assessing eyes remained. "Can you pick up Watts's trail again once we get past this mess?"

Ethan splayed his hands at his waist, opening up his chest to take in a deep, fortifying breath, giving Ben a chance to do the same. So far, their solitary hike up Ute Mountain had been an endurance trek that burned through the muscles in his legs. But from what he could see, the real climb was about to begin. Automatically checking the gear strapped to his vest, belt and pack, he swept his gaze back and forth, up and down, familiarizing himself with the changes in the landscape.

"I think so." He nodded toward the split in the rocks about forty yards ahead where the softer sandstone on either side of the gray granite outcropping had eroded away to form a natural fork in the trail. Going up and over the granite would lead them to Rising Sun Creek and the summit beyond, while climbing down would take them into the gorge and onto the narrow or possibly nonexistent riverbank.

Unfortunately, between their location and the fork in the rocks lay forty yards of do-not-try-this-at-home terrain. Gravelly soil and a few larger boulders had tumbled down with the trees, obscuring the path worn by wild animals, a few intrepid hunters and hikers—and most likely—one whiskey-steeped, resourceful fugitive on the run.

"You don't say much, do you, Bia?" Ben teased. "Don't tell me we're turning back."

"Wouldn't think of it." Ethan unhooked a rope and a clip of carabiners and tossed them to the FBI agent. "But we are going to tie ourselves off before we cross here." He glanced over the broken treetops below them. "That's a mighty long way to fall if you do miss that step."

Ethan secured a rope around his waist and looped his climbing hammer around his wrist before moving through the fallen trees and crawling up the steep, crumbling incline to find solid rock where he could anchor a series of pitons and run a guide rope through. He rode the miniature slide of loose gravel his descent created back down to Agent Parrish and secured his rope to the mountain face, as well.

"Ready? We're going up and over the slide. Remember to sit back on the line and walk up the slope. Step where I do."

Ben pulled his rope taut. "Lead on, MacDuff."

Twenty-five painstaking minutes later, they'd reached the fork in the rock. Ethan had broken out into a sweat and Ben was visibly breathing harder. He ordered the agent to take another drink while he secured their lines.

"You think Watts got caught in this mess?" Ben asked, sucking his water bottle dry.

"No way to know until I scout up ahead." Ethan inspected the diverging paths, running his hands and eyes along the crags and lichens of the bluff wall, and stooping down to search the scrub vegetation that clung to the rock face leading down to the river, looking for signs left by man, not nature. "I haven't seen any evidence of scavengers, or vultures overhead. They'd find a dead or wounded man before we would."

"You're a laugh a minute, big guy. You want me to radio in our progress? What the hell…?"

Ethan felt the first cold drop on his cheek even before he glanced back to see Ben's upturned hand.

"Rain?"

"Rain." Ethan took note of the slightly pale cast to Ben Parrish's skin. Tough was tough, but even *he* was beginning to feel the exertion of their ascent. Sherman Watts had taken two days to climb the ground they were covering in one. Rather than push Ben so far that he wound up collapsing from exhaustion, Ethan ordered a longer break. "Call it in. Tell Bart that we've reached Cougar Fork. Martinez will know where we are." A line of thick clouds rolled over the sun overhead, casting the late afternoon into twilight and darkening the shadows among the trees. "Tell them we're staying the night. Unless we find Watts and need the helicopter to fly us out, we'll resume contact at first light."

"Will do. Ute Base—this is Scout One. Ute Base, come in." Static crackled over the radio in response. "Damn. Have we lost the frequency?"

"The weather must be interfering. Try another channel."

Ben nodded, turning the volume down, adjusting the reception through a series of piercing pitches, trying to find a working band. "I'll ask if Bart can soup up the power at his end so we don't lose contact."

Ethan took a few steps along the lower path. There was plenty of mud and enough foliage in the crevasse to mark the tracks of a group of foxes—probably a mother and her kits. But nothing human. As he suspected, Watts's trail meant they had more mountain to climb.

Ben tinkered with controls until the shrill tones narrowed into silence. "Bingo." He raised the two-way radio to his mouth again. "Ute Base—this is Scout One. Do you read?"

"Scout One—this is Ute Base." Bart Flemming's voice sounded small and distant. "You sound like you're all the way down in New Mexico. What…your position?"

"Cougar Fork." Ben raised his voice to be heard. "Hey, Bart. Can you work some of your magic from that end? You're breaking up. Could be the atmosphere with this storm. How hard is it going to hit us?"

"The Weather Bureau…" While Bart and Ben exchanged and repeated pertinent information, Ethan explored a few yards ahead.

Lightning streaked across the sky, and for the next half a moment, reception completely cut out. In that one beat of silence, Ethan heard it.

The crunch of gravel beneath a foot.

Thunder rumbled. Static answered, masking the sound. Another man might think he'd imagined it.

"Be apprised, Agent…arrived." Then more static.

"Sounds like Tom and Dylan and your men are back at camp." Ben stood as he relayed the message to Ethan and signed off. "Ute Base—this is Scout One. Out."

The radio crackled. The sky rumbled. Ethan braced his feet and closed his eyes and listened to the world, sorting through the sounds around him.

"I hate to say it, big guy, but we may be incommunicado until after this storm—"

Ethan raised a fist beside his ear and Ben instantly

fell silent. He turned to meet the agent's eyes. Good. *Their* communication was clear.

Man approaching.

In one smooth, noiseless movement, Ben set the radio on the ground beside his pack and pulled his gun.

Ethan pointed down the path to the gorge, indicating the direction from which the footstep had sounded. He could hear them clearly now. The steps were soft, steady, slow to approach.

Their unsuspecting quarry was coming to them.

He wasn't on a battlefield, and Ben wasn't a soldier under his command, but the two of them instantly reacted as though they'd suddenly found themselves in enemy territory.

After exchanging a few cryptic hand signals, Ben retreated behind a stand of scrub pines while Ethan hoisted himself up onto the rocky ledge overhanging the path. Drawing his knife and turning it in his fist, he crouched low and waited for their man to appear.

Come on, Watts, he urged silently. *Let's get this damn mission over with and get you back to Joanna.*

Lightning split the sky overhead, charging every nerve, flashing in his retinas. The answering thunder ripped through the air, loud and fierce, right on top of them.

The footsteps neared. Slowed. Retreated.

Damn. Watts must have heard a sound or—hell, Ben's gear was right there in the middle of the path. Watts must have seen it.

Ethan didn't wait to find out if that click and whisper of sound was a gun being drawn.

He jumped.

Springing like a mountain lion from his perch, Ethan

tackled the tall figure that crept beneath him. With a startled "oof," their visitor went down. They hit the ground hard, rolled, smacked into the rocks.

Watts wasn't about to make this easy. With a growl, he twisted beneath Ethan, a sharp elbow catching him in the gut. Something harder clipped him in the chin. The blow rang through Ethan's skull. And in the moment it took to blink the dots of light from his eyes, Watts grabbed his wrist and shoved the knife away.

Ben charged their position, gun drawn. "FBI! Drop your weapon!"

"Oh, my God… E—"

Enough! Watts was fast for an older man. Scrappy. Tough. But Ethan was stronger. And that hellish night Joanna had been raped was still so fresh on his mind…

"Ethan! Bia!" Ben Parrish was shouting at *him.* "Back it off!"

Ethan flicked the knife into the brush and shifted his grip to pin his opponent's wrist. He captured the other wrist and knocked it against the ground. Once. Twice, dislodging the gun Watts had clobbered him with. He pinned that wrist.

"Ethan?"

His opponent had gone slack in his grip, giving him an easy advantage. He kicked the perp's legs apart, pinned the left leg. Pinned the right.

"Ethan," his slender attacker wheezed. "Please!"

The haze of adrenaline cleared his system enough to recognize that precious voice. It took another second to focus in on the man spread-eagled beneath him.

Not a man.

Breasts—small, pert, proud—thrust up to meet every

deep breath of his chest, again and again as his captive breathed in deeply, trying to catch *her* breath.

Hell. Oh, hell.

Ethan looked down into deep brown eyes and a swath of midnight-colored hair, tangled with pine needles, mud and gravel.

He'd attacked the very thing he'd so fiercely wanted to protect.

Joanna.

"DID I HURT YOU?" Joanna asked, brushing the muck and gravel off her jeans as she bent to retrieve her weapon. Just as quickly as Ethan had leaped from the heavens and tackled her, he'd rolled off her and put a good ten feet of space between them.

"I'm sorry, *Nüa-rü.* I'm sorry. I had that knife... What you must have thought..." His black-eyed gaze swung over to Ben Parrish and Ethan fell silent.

She could well imagine where Ethan's thoughts had gone. For a split second, she'd gone back to that night, too. But for only a split second. She'd had fifteen years of self-defense training to make the instinct to fight back second nature. Yes, a man had forced her down. Had held a knife to her throat. Had even trapped her in that completely vulnerable position beneath the heavier weight of his body. She hadn't allowed herself the time to think of the rape, to compare, to fear. She'd simply fought for her freedom.

Now she was fighting to reassure the one man who might give a damn that he'd reminded her of that most painful chapter of her life.

"I'm okay, Ethan. Are you?" Did he understand that

she meant more than physical pain? Ignoring the twinge in her wrist from having it pummeled against the ground, she holstered her Glock and tried to read beneath the stoic mask of Ethan's face. "You jumped me from behind. For all I knew, you could have been Watts. I had to defend myself."

He scraped his palm over his jaw, wiping the moisture from his face. Yep. The spot where she'd clocked him with her gun was going to leave a mark on his tanned skin. "What part of 'stay put' don't you understand?"

Okay. Anger.

She curbed the impulse to snap back with a *What part of "you're not the boss of me" don't* you *understand?* His anger was justified, and not unexpected. Knowing that she seemed to be the only one who could elicit that particular emotion in the normally gentle giant added another brick onto the weight of guilt she carried where Ethan was concerned.

Verbally duking it out in front of an audience wouldn't have been her first choice, but at least Agent Parrish had the decency to look utterly focused on radioing in her location to Bart Flemming down at the base camp. She was safe. All search party members had been accounted for.

Joanna had been exhausted by her climb, but wrestling with Ethan had fired enough adrenaline through her system to give her renewed energy. She blinked the rain from her eyelashes and took a step toward him, but halted when his chiseled jaw clenched and he turned away. Fine, she'd give her explanation from here. "When Dylan Acevedo and his guide returned to base camp without any success, I knew I couldn't sit there or in my hotel room, waiting for someone to call and tell me Watts had slipped through your manhunt. It sounds as though Agent Ryan and Garan Coons are back at camp now, too."

"I sent them back for their own safety."

Right on cue, lightning sparked on and off like a strobe in the sky. Joanna jumped as the clap of thunder, amplified by the altitude, followed just a couple of seconds later. She understood that if the lightning came much closer, exposed on the mountainside like this, they'd make prime targets for a strike.

Did the man think he was invincible? That he was so one with nature that the storm would somehow spare him? She ignored the invisible fortress of solitude he'd erected around himself and crossed right up to him. "You're in danger up here, too. How is it okay for you to worry about the rest of us, but I can't worry about you?"

And she had been worried. But that wasn't what this discussion was about, apparently.

"Parrish and I have Watts's trail. He'll be forced to take shelter on the mountain tonight, too." With a sigh that sounded almost as if he was disgusted that he couldn't keep himself from touching her, Ethan plucked a twig from her hair and tossed it to the ground. "There's no reason for anyone else to risk their lives when we're this close to catching up to him."

"You can't leave me behind. This case is too important to me." Would he welcome *her* touch if she reached up and brushed away the debris that clung to the nappy collar of his green-and-tan flannel shirt? The instinct was there, but she fought off giving in to the temptation.

Instead, she busied her hands by unhooking her fraying ponytail and smoothing all the damp, wayward strands around her face. She bound them back into place at the back of her head. "There's nothing for me to do down at base camp. Flemming is monitoring all the communications and coordinating with the crime unit. I told Martinez I was familiar with the area and wanted to do some exploring on my own and he okayed it."

"He let you come up here without a survival pack or radio?"

She wasn't a fool. "I took my pack off and left it on the trail up to the fork when I heard a man's voice up here. I wanted to be able to defend myself if I needed to. Looks like I did."

"Does he know how far you were planning on going? How dangerous it is to hike along the river with it cresting like it is? Night's falling. The storm's almost here. You could have been injured or kidnapped, or just have gotten lost, and no one would have known it."

"I'm not going to sit down there and twiddle my thumbs when I can be doing something useful up here."

"You don't think I can do my job?"

"I'm not implying that."

"The hell you aren't, Superwoman. You can't give up control of one damn thing, can you? You can't trust anyone to do you a favor or help with your job or... protect you." He hunched down to bring his face eye level with hers, dropping his voice to a low-pitched whisper. "Accepting help is not a sign of weakness. It doesn't mean you're going to fall apart or fail or be hurt if you can't control every last detail of your life."

Joanna frowned. "Is that really how you see me?"

"Am I wrong?" He straightened to his full height, forcing her to tilt her chin to read every nuance of his next taunt. "Tell me exactly who you trust, Joanna. Give me a list of names of people you rely on without question."

The wind picked up, splashing cold raindrops across her upturned face. But Joanna couldn't look away. She was too stunned to realize how much she hated—how much it hurt—that he was right.

"I didn't think so." He spun around, spotted his knife at the roots of a gnarled pine bush and strode over to reclaim his weapon.

She followed on his heels, forgetting for a moment that they had an audience. "Who the hell was I ever going to count on, Ethan? My parents? The family friend who raped me? The sheriff who let him get away with it?"

But Ethan hadn't forgotten the other agent who was with them. "Ben. Pack your gear and climb on up to that next ledge. There are some caves up there where we can take shelter for the night. Make sure there aren't any visitors before you go in. The snakes and smaller predators will be looking for a warm, dry place, too."

"Got it. You two, um, take your time."

From the corner of her eye, she saw Ben gear up and disappear above the granite overhang. But her gaze was glued to Ethan, as she waited for an answer, waited for understanding.

When he faced her again, the anger was gone. Something ancient and hard and cynical had replaced it. "How about the man who loves you? You ever think about giving him a chance? Trusting him?"

"Don't say that."

"What? Don't throw my pride to the wind and beg

you to let me back into your life? Or don't…?" He shook his head, uttered a sound that was not quite a laugh. "Hell. Haven't you figured it out? I never got over Joanna Kuchu. Once the big guy fell, it stuck."

"No."

But it was there, clearly stamped on his honest, care-worn features. It was the love they'd once shared—twisted and neglected and beaten down into something far different than the innocent hope and endless desire they'd found in each other at eighteen and twenty-one.

A shiver—of guilt and sorrow and the love she missed trying to break through—rippled down her spine. "I'm sorry, Ethan. I'm just not that girl anymore."

"You don't want to feel a thing, do you? You're the uncompromising lady FBI agent. All business. All the time. You even changed your name to erase a past that didn't fit in with this newer, tougher version of you." He gentled his tone, but the truth of his words was still hard to stomach. "You don't want to let another person in because you're afraid Joanna Kuchu will get hurt again."

She pressed her lips together in a thin, taut line, afraid of what might come out if she tried to answer.

"That's real strength, *Nüa-rü*. To love. To trust. To allow yourself to need someone." He stuffed that long, wicked knife back inside its sheath and tied it off with the leather cord at the top. As her emotions were surfacing, his appeared to be shutting down. "Someday, I hope you find that again. I hope you find friends. And someone who's more than a friend. Your life's going to be empty until you do. And that…truly breaks my heart."

The sky opened up and the rain beat down like the relentless chill in her heart. His words had broken down some indefinable barrier, fracturing her carefully structured world. But she tried to piece together what she could. "What do you want me to say? That I loved you once? I did. Maybe a part of me still does because it…hurts…to know how badly I hurt you." She swiped the rain from her face, taking with it the tears she didn't want to cry. "But I have to be the way I am. That's how I handled my parents and rape and recovery. That's how I got through Quantico. That's how I'll get up this mountain and do my job and get back to my life in D.C."

"I'm sure Joanna Rhodes will handle it all just fine." He nodded toward the rock face that Agent Parrish had climbed. "Go on. You're next." He picked up his backpack and waited for her at the base of the wall. "Watch your step. It'll be slick."

"That's it?" End of discussion? Climb the wall? "You're not sending me back to base camp?"

He tested a couple of handholds, and tugged at one protrusion about a foot above his head. "Grab on here. This one's solid." When she didn't immediately move to obey, he circled behind her, planted his hands at her waist and lifted her onto the wall in front of him. "I don't like the idea of you being alone in the same room with Watts when armed guards and hidden cameras are watching his every move. I sure as hell don't want you running into him out here in the wild where he has the advantage."

Joanna automatically tightened her grip and secured her feet. When she shook the rain from her eyes and pulled herself up to the next handhold, he released her. The warmth of his hands and his unreadable mood remained. "I'm not here to be a burden, Ethan. I would think another set of eyes and another gun up here would be welcome. I never asked you to protect me from Watts."

"Get your ass up that mountain. And don't you leave my sight."

While Joanna Rhodes resisted the order, some little part of her that was still Joanna Kuchu warmed at the growly declaration that she was now part of the team. And that Ethan Bia, in some skewed way, still cared.

She tested the next grip, found a pool of slimy mud and hunted for the next hole or protrusion where she could grab on. The next one wasn't deep enough. "I don't see where..."

Ethan was on the climb beside her now. He reached for her hand and pulled it closer. "Here."

He cupped her fingers over a knob of granite. Following his example, Joanna shifted her weight and pulled herself up another foot. But she stopped abruptly. "I forgot my pack down—"

Boom!

A deafening noise exploded overhead. With her breath startled from her lungs, Joanna instinctively hugged the rock face. "Was that thunder?"

Only if lightning had struck the bluff above them.

Maybe it had. A low hum, like the distant reverberation of running hooves, rumbled overhead. The spatter of raindrops became the clacking of tiny gravel sprinkling down over the face of the rock. Joanna tipped her face up as the hoofbeats crescendoed into a stampede of a thousand buffalo charging straight toward them. The granite itself shook beneath her hands.

"Ethan?"

"Move!" Ethan snaked his arm around Joanna's waist and leaped.

The first pebble thunked off her scalp as Ethan shoved her beneath the overhang and sandwiched her against the granite wall, shielding her with his body. Joanna grabbed two fistfuls of his vest and shirts and buried her face against his chest as the mountain came down on top of them.

Chapter Seven

"Joanna."

The voice against her ear was as soothing as the solid thump of the heartbeat beneath her hand. She felt drowsy and warm and content.

"Joanna." The voice was slightly more urgent this time, rousing her to the bruising rocks poking into her back and bottom. She tried to squirm away from the discomfort.

"*Nüa-rü.* You okay?" Hard hands, running along her body from shoulders to hips and up into her hair, probing for injury, chased away the last of her shocked stupor. The rock slide. They'd survived.

"Ethan?" She lifted her head and inhaled a deep breath, but wound up with a noseful of dust that triggered a coughing spasm.

"Easy." The rough pads of Ethan's thumbs stroked across her eyes and nose and lips. Moist, tender kisses followed every touch—to an eyelid, the corner of her mouth, the tip of her nose—offering comfort and stirring memories after wiping away the dirt and debris that seemed to cover every part of them. When the coughing passed and her airways had cleared, he framed her jaw between his hands and inspected her with his eyes. "Better?"

Even with the shadows of rocks and rain and the encroaching night, his eyes seemed to pierce the darkness with a light from within. It was a light she could cling to when the world was literally falling down around her. It was a light that could guide her to safety. If she let it.

"I'm okay." She released her death grip on the front of his vest and reached up to brush small chunks of rock off his shoulders. His face needed a wipe of her hands, too. She ran her thumbs along the creases from sun and laughter beside his eyes, and cleared the dirt from the stern line of his mouth. "Are you hurt?"

"Some bruises, maybe. Nothing serious."

"Same here." The rain beyond Ethan's back was already tamping down the rising dust as the last few bits of rolling rock settled into their new resting places. "Looks like I *did* need you. You saved my life. Thank you."

"Anytime. See? That wasn't so hard, was it?"

She shook her head. Allowing herself to need him, just this once, hadn't been hard at all.

His striking black hair had been coated with a mix of ruddy red and gray debris. Even as she combed her fingertips through the short, damp silk, she was imagining a picture of what he might look like forty years from now—or after a can of paint had spilled on his head. The thought of an elegantly aged Ethan, or one who might be klutzy enough to make mistakes like she did, curved her lips into a smile. Her smile seemed to please him, relax him. The hands that had framed her face were suddenly sliding around her waist, pulling her closer. He bent his head, his lips hovering over hers.

"That would have crushed us. Sent us over the edge of the mountain. I could have lost you again."

The almost moment of shared tenderness vanished in unison. How long had they been standing there? Seconds? Minutes?

Joanna said it first. "Agent Parrish."

"Ben!"

Ethan was already moving, hauling himself out of the recess where they'd taken shelter, onto the new incline of rubble that had completely wiped away the path to Cougar Fork. As Joanna dug herself a toehold in the crumbled rock, Ethan reached down and clamped his hand around her wrist, pulling her right along with him as he climbed.

"Ahh!" She winced at the dull ache that throbbed in her arm.

He set her on her feet beside him and immediately released her. "You *are* hurt."

She brushed aside the hands that probed the scrapes and red marks encircling her wrist and wiggled all her fingers, showing him it was just sore, nothing broken. "It's from our wrestling match earlier."

"I'm sorry. I should have waited to see—"

"Go." She tried to turn him, urge him on up the slope ahead of her. "Find Ben. I'll get there."

"*We'll* get there." Moving and making promises all at once, he switched his grip to her other hand. The ground beneath them shifted like a giant pile of sand beneath every step, but he helped her reach the wide ledge of the bluff far more quickly than she could have managed on her own. But once they reached the relatively flat surface high above the river, he released her and went into search mode. "Ben! Can you hear me?"

"Ben!" she echoed.

There was less debris here, but still enough loose boulders and larger rock to pick through. Ethan jogged ahead, checking the entrance to one shallow cave and then the next.

Joanna's feet followed her gaze to the edge of the bluff where dusty treetops and other plant life sprouted from the jagged wall that dropped down to the Silverton River. She peered over the rim and visually skimmed small ledges and roots and tree trunks where a strong man might still be clinging to life.

"Ben!" Though she could hear the river roaring past below her, the rain and darkness prevented her from seeing all the way down to the water. She glanced over her shoulder, following the pyramid of rubble to the next rise above them where the slide had started. Nothing but dark clouds and flashes of lightning and more rock. Could he have gotten up there before the mountain gave way and swept him over the edge into the gorge? A sinking feeling gnawed in her stomach as she looked back to the chasm below her. "You don't think he...?"

"Over here!"

Clinging to a renewed surge of hope, Joanna hurried over to a depression in the bluff wall where Ethan was lifting softball-size rocks and tossing them aside. She joined him in his excavation efforts, scraping aside armloads of mud and gravel until the entire pile of rubble bowed out and sank back in, as if the mountain itself were breathing.

"Ben?" She called to the man she could hear cursing and grunting and clearing rock from the opposite side.

Two more rocks. A little more gravel. Then a gritty

hand poked through. An arm followed. And then Ethan was pulling her back as the remaining pile collapsed and Ben Parrish emerged from the cave where he'd been buried alive.

"Oh, man." On apparently steady legs, he climbed out of his hidey-hole and swatted the dirt from his jeans and fatigue sweater. The white *FBI* letters on the Kevlar he wore had been dusted a dull, brownish gray. "That was exciting," he drawled.

Like Ethan, Joanna checked his light brown eyes for clarity and scanned him from head to toe for any signs of injury beyond the nicks and scrapes on his hands. If she could believe appearances, her fellow agent had survived in one piece. "Good thing you had that cave you could take cover in. Were you injured?"

Ethan had already completed that assessment and had a very different sort of question for him. "Could you pinpoint the source of the blast?"

Blast? Joanna's eyes widened. "You mean that rock slide was man-made?"

Ben nodded and apologized at the same time. "Almost straight above us. I'm going out on a limb and confirming that Watts stole some C-4 along with that truck." He summoned them both to follow him back over the pile of rubble into the cave that turned out to be about the size of her apartment's bedroom back in D.C. "This is a lot deeper than the others, thought I'd found a dry place for the night. I was heading inside when I hit a damn trip wire buried in the dirt across the opening." The two men squatted beside what was left of a filament that had been partially covered by the slide. "Looks like we don't just have the weather to contend with anymore. Watts has booby-trapped his trail."

Meanwhile, Joanna had pulled out her flashlight and was staring at the roof of the cave. The granite was gray, with bits of quartz and other sediment impurities sparkling with the reflection of her light. But there was one spot that was grayer, duller, than the rest of the cave. Joanna indicated the spot with her light. "Could this have been Watts's camp last night? There's evidence of smoke from a fire. I don't know how to tell if it's recent, though."

"It's recent," Ethan stated unequivocally. Joanna turned her light to the spot where he was digging in the dirt. He held up a palmful of dark, gravelly mud for her and Ben to inspect. "This ground has been freshly turned. Ashes from a wood fire have been mixed in." He squeezed the mud into a clump and tossed it at his feet as he stood. "I'd say Watts is covering his tracks in more ways than one."

Her pulse quickened with a jolt of anticipation. "So we're closing in on him?"

Ben reminded them that they weren't the only ones interested in capturing Sherman Watts. "I'll radio it in. Looks like we may need backup after all."

The rain seemed to wash away the dust that coated Ben almost as soon as he pulled the two-way from his pack and stepped outside. "Ute Base—this is Scout One. Ute Base, come in—do you read?" Static crackled. "I need to move farther away from the rocks to see if they can pick me up. "Ute Base—this is Scout One."

Joanna turned her attention back to Ethan, and waited for an answer. "Can you still find him? Or has this explosion obliterated any trace of him?"

His dark eyes didn't offer the immediate assurance she was used to seeing. "I don't know. I need to think this through. Maybe in the daylight—"

A distinctive pop of sound jerked through Joanna's body. She didn't have to hear the second shot, or the one after that, to pull her weapon and dive for cover.

Gunfire.

And they were the targets.

"DAMN IT, ETHAN, let go!"

Ethan had ducked behind the pile of rubble with Joanna, tugging on the back of her belt to hold her down beside him as she crawled to the top to try to pin down the shooter's position. "The shots are coming from above us."

"Exactly. We're sitting ducks down here."

She wiggled out of his protective grasp. "Then let me do my job." She spotted Agent Parrish first, running toward the edge of the bluff, firing blindly behind him. "Ben?"

"Under fire. Repeat, we are under fire!" His body jerked and he cursed. The radio smashed to the ground.

He was an open target.

When Joanna saw the circle of red blooming on the sleeve of his sweater, she knew she had to help him. "He's hit!"

Joanna scrambled down the other side of the rock pile and raised her gun to the flatland above the caves. From this angle, she couldn't make out the shooter, but that didn't matter. She could back him away from the edge. Keep him from getting close enough to shoot in this direction. She could protect Ben.

Steady. Breathe out. Squeeze the trigger.

Squinting against the rain assaulting her vision, she

fired off round after round, emptying her gun into the abyss above them, hopefully laying enough cover fire for Ben to drop down to a ledge or duck behind a boulder for safety. When her clip was spent, she fell back against the rocks and ejected her magazine.

But when she reached for the spare clip on her belt, Ethan's hands were already there, pushing the fresh ammo into her hand. "What are you doing? You're unarmed. Stay put."

"Like that command ever worked with you. Ben took one in the chest."

Joanna's heart sank. "No."

"It hit him in the Kevlar, but he went over the edge."

"Unless he caught a ledge or tree, that's at least thirty feet to the ground."

"Or the river." To her horror, Ethan wrapped her fingers around the magazine of bullets and squeezed her hand. He pointed out the silence overhead. "He's reloading. Cover me."

"Ethan!"

As quick as a coiled snake, he bolted behind a nearby boulder, then zigzagged out to a smaller one. The shots overhead started again, changed direction, zeroed in on Ethan's position. There was nothing more between him and the other side of that ledge big enough to hide behind. *Oh, hell.*

"Do it, girl." Joanna urged herself into action, locking the clip into place and sliding the first bullet into the chamber. "Now!"

Between the thunder and her gun and the shooter above, it was the loudest thirty seconds of Joanna's life.

"Ethan?" She wasn't the only one who'd stopped

firing when her clip was spent, but when she looked out across the outcropping of granite, she saw she was alone. She raised her voice. "Ethan? Where are you? Are you all right?"

He must have gone over the edge, as well. But on purpose, or… "Don't go there."

What she wouldn't give for clear skies and daylight. But she couldn't even risk shining her flashlight out there and giving their attacker—Watts, she presumed—a clear target.

"Don't be dead," she mouthed. "Please, God, don't be dead."

Huddled against the rocks at the base of the cliff, she squeezed her eyes shut and tried to listen to the world the way Ethan did, the way he'd taught her to all those years ago. She heard thunder, wild and deafening, up in the sky and rattling through the air around her. She heard her own crazy heartbeat, hammering in her ears. The wind whooshed past her. The rain pummeled the ground.

Or were those footsteps? The rustling of movement in the trees beyond the ledge? Or…it was no good. Her ears were still ringing from all the noise of the shootout. She couldn't even tell if the movement was real or imaginary, much less whether or not it came from above or below her.

"Think this through, Joanna." She climbed back over the top of the rubble and rolled down the other side into the cave, keeping a low profile until she was certain the danger had passed.

Her gun was empty; she had no more ammo. Ben was wounded, Ethan was missing and she was alone. That was the way she liked it, right? Alone? She'd built up her strength by learning to think and do for herself. Self-reliance was the only way to keep the Sherman Wattses of the world from having any power over her again.

But Ethan's share-your-strength-to-build-your-strength philosophy had gotten into her head and she couldn't seem to make clear choices and know her own mind the way she did back in D.C. Away from this place. Away from Watts.

Away from Ethan.

A purely emotional reaction, gut deep and as true as anything she'd ever known, chased away her logic. She had to go out there. She had to see if Ethan was all right. Ben, too.

But first, she had to secure the scene. Fears aside, she had to protect both men. To do that, she needed a weapon. Using her gun as a steel club again wouldn't be her first choice, but…

Ben Parrish.

She flipped on her light and searched the cave for Ben's backpack. "Yes."

She grabbed the pack and unclipped the top, turning it over to dump out the contents. He carried a bureau-issue Glock like her own. If he wasn't wearing it when he'd gone over the cliff, he'd have a spare magazine she could use. After she pulled out a reflective hypothermia blanket, water bottles and energy bars, other survival gear tumbled out—along with an entire box of 9 mm bullets. "That'll do."

As she sat down to restock both magazines, clip one onto her belt and load the other into her gun, she wondered just what kind of confrontation Ben had been expecting with Watts—or if the wisecracking agent was one of those macho men who simply hated to travel light. Either way, his excess was to her advantage, and she was on her way up and over the rubble that masked the cave opening.

Tucking her gun into the back of her belt for instant access, Joanna slid along the cliff wall until she reached the unaltered rock beyond the blast area above the cave. Then she turned and began to climb, searching for the holes and bumps and recesses in the granite where she could find a grip or place a toe. Her muscles were feeling the strain of the arduous day, and her bruised wrist ached each time she pulled her weight with her right arm.

Soon after she crested the top and crept over to inspect the area above the caves, Joanna realized that their attacker had abandoned his position. She recognized the path that could lead her on up to Rising Sun Creek, which was where Watts had most likely run off to hide. Instead of maintaining the pursuit on her own, she followed her nose in the opposite direction, to the source of the sulfuric odor of gunpowder lingering in the air. In addition to dozens of metal casings scattered across the rocks, an empty bottle of generic-label whiskey marked the dip where he must have lain. He would have been almost completely protected from every direction but the sky, and had a clear view of the outer ledge below.

Odd. "I thought Jack Daniel's was your brand."

She supposed a fugitive with little money in his pocket couldn't afford to be choosy. But then, she wouldn't have suspected that Sherman Watts would position himself like a sniper and take potshots at federal agents, either. Blowing up a mountain to cover his tracks so he could hide out like the weasel he was, accepting whatever collateral damage occurred, she could believe. But intentionally firing a kill shot at Ben Parrish?

Quit profiling. Help Ethan.

Joanna pocketed three of the casings for comparison later, but left the bottle. She wasn't up here to collect evidence. If Watts was gone, the scene was secure. Time to find Ethan and Ben. She climbed back down as quickly as slippery grips and sticky, rain-soaked clothes would allow.

"Ethan?" she shouted once more into the darkness, but the storm swallowed up the uneasy concern of her voice. "Where the hell are you, big guy?" she whispered.

"Is it clear?" Though it sounded as though it had come from miles away, Joanna swung her flashlight around, instantly drawn to the deep pitch of his voice. She saw a pair of big hands gripping the edge of the outcropping where Ben Parrish had fallen.

"We're clear!"

If that was a sniffle of relief, she ignored it. She was too busy running. "Ethan!"

A long, muscular leg appeared, hooking itself over the granite lip, and he pulled himself up onto the ledge.

Joanna was on her knees, dragging him back from the edge of the precipice, looking for anything more than the tear in his shirtsleeve or the scrape on his elbow to indicate he'd been hurt. When he pushed up onto his hands, Joanna tugged on his gear vest to help him sit up. She wound her arms around his neck and hugged him tight, his chest heaving in and out against her stomach as he struggled to catch his breath. His hands settled at her hips. The strength of his grip indicated he was tired, but he was holding on. He felt strong and solid and safe.

She kissed his temple. Kissed the chiseled angle of his cheek. She pulled back just far enough to press a hard kiss to his mouth. His fingers found a renewed strength, turning to stretch down to the curve of her bottom, to squeeze, to claim, to lift her to his mouth for another kiss.

"Lord, woman. You'd think I'd been gone fifteen years instead of fifteen minutes."

"Don't be sarcastic. That's not you, Ethan. I was scared you'd been shot."

"Shh. I'm in one piece."

She hugged him again, needing the reassurance that his body was whole and unharmed by feeling its warmth and vitality with her own. "I found the shooter's position, but I don't know. Something's not right. I don't want to think that…" The stillness that engulfed him finally registered. He was breathing deeply and evenly; his heart had steadied into a healthy rhythm. But the line of his mouth was grim as she pulled back. "What's wrong?"

He rested one hand on her thigh. With the other, he pulled a wet strand of hair from her cheek and smoothed it all the way back to the band of her ponytail. "I know I promised to find him for you, but we have to let Watts go tonight."

Don't say it.

"I climbed all the way down to the rocks by the river. I can't find Ben. Not even a body."

Joanna touched his face, cupped his jaw the way she once had every time she greeted him or said goodbye. He seemed to need her reassurance, her forgiveness, even. She nodded her understanding. "I'll help you look for him. You said the second shot hit him in the vest. The first hit was an arm wound. Neither is fatal. If he didn't land on his head, he could have survived the fall."

"He could have been swept away by the river."

"And he could just be lost in the dark. We'll find him."

After a long silent moment, Ethan turned his lips into her palm and pressed a kiss there. "Look at you having hope." He nodded, approving, maybe even finding a little hope of his own to cling to. "Okay." The vacuum of energy surrounding him dissipated and he rolled to his feet, catching Joanna's hand and pulling her up beside him. "I'll scrounge up what gear I can. There's no way down to the river from this side except over the bluff now."

"Watts can wait." She found herself agreeing, and meaning it. "I'll call it in. We'll get helicopters and lights out here as soon as the storm has passed. We'll get all the help we need."

Her search for Ben's radio ended quickly.

They weren't getting any help after all.

The radio had been shot to pieces.

Chapter Eight

"It's definitely blood."

Ethan held his fingers out to the spray coming off the river that raced just below his feet and let it wash the sticky red goo from his fingers. He might be trailing a wounded animal as easily as a wounded man—if all he had to go on were the fading drops he'd found on the lee side of this cone-shaped boulder. But he'd never known any animal up on Ute Mountain to leave its blood trail in the shape of a partial handprint wrapped around the trunk of a small tree.

With a pair of flashlights to light the bluff on his second trip down, Ethan had been able to see where the roots of a small pine had ripped from the shallow, waterlogged soil. Ben Parrish must have grabbed on to it as he fell. The weakened tree couldn't catch him, but it must have held tight long enough to slow his descent and break his fall at the bottom.

Now, ten yards away, Ethan had found the second bloodstain. Ben must have stumbled straight into the river.

"With his injury, he might not have been able to make the climb back up." Joanna had to shout to be heard over the thunder of the water. "Or maybe with the shooting still going on, he swam across and went to get help."

Ethan threw out his arm like a crossing guard when Joanna slipped on the bank's muddy slope. She caught herself, ignored his arm and squatted down to shine her light on the blood. She was perfectly fine without his help. But the need to protect her was more powerful than ever. The worry that he might not be strong enough or smart enough or aware enough to provide that protection when she needed him most was just as troublesome.

Because it was just the two of them now. Just the two of them alone on the mountain like those long, balmy summer nights they'd shared when they were younger and more innocent. Like the night when he'd spread a blanket on a flowery knoll and they'd made love for the first time, under the stars.

Only this wasn't summer. The weather sucked. And there was nothing innocent about fugitives and explosions and missing, wounded FBI agents.

Though she probably didn't need his help getting up, either, Ethan still slipped his hand beneath her arm when she started to rise. He kept it there to turn her back up the slope.

But she planted her feet and tilted her chin. "Aren't we going across to see if we can pick up his trail on the other side?"

"No." He nudged. She balked.

"We're both strong swimmers. And it's not that wide."

"It's not the distance. It's the speed of the current and the rocks hidden below that worry me. We're not swimming in that death trap, period." That little dimple of a frown appeared on her forehead, and he could see the urge to argue the point with him flashing in her eyes. Surprise, surprise. But this was a small battle in the grand scheme of *discussions* they'd shared since her arrival some thirty-six hours ago. Why fight it? "There's a natural bridge about a mile down where we can cross."

The frown disappeared. "And then we can come back this far on the opposite bank to see if there's any sign that Ben climbed out on the other side."

She headed on out before he even reached the top of the bank. In a wave of sheer orneriness, fueled by a growing fatigue that was wearing down his keep-it-patient-and-polite filters, Ethan raised the beam of his light to the sweet sway of her tush. Now, *that* was the one piece of scenery he'd missed since coming back to Colorado. Yeah, that was a view he could follow all night long.

And judging by the pace Joanna set on the narrow but relatively flat strip of land, he just might have to. But he wasn't about to be outtracked by some wannabe city girl from Washington, D.C.

Night had fallen. Lightning flickered in the clouds overhead as the storm moved on and left a soft, steady rain in its wake. Ethan lengthened his stride and quickly caught up to Joanna. "You know, we could wait until dawn to continue the search. Or at least until the rain ends and we get some moonlight to guide us."

"If *I* was the one who fell over that cliff, would you wait for moonlight?" *She* was the one he was trying to look out for. If he was this tired, she must be running on fumes. "Besides, the land here runs through your veins. I bet you could track someone blindfolded if you had to."

He grunted a laugh. "I'm good. But I'm not that good."

"Don't be so modest, big guy. I think that's why you feel so at home here on the reservation and around the Four Corners area. You feel the earth and its secrets and power in your blood." Yet she never had, despite her curiosity to learn everything he had to teach. He'd always felt so settled, so strong here, whereas she'd been determined—destined, even—to move on. That's why he'd nicknamed her "the wind." *Nüa-rü* inhaled a deep breath before tilting a shy smile up to him. "That was one of the things that fascinated me about you when we first met. I remember when your brother, Kyle, bragged that you knew every rock and stalk of grass on Ute Mountain. I thought he was exaggerating, of course. I remember that first Saturday—Mother and Dad had chewed me out for not coming up with the money to bail them out of jail the night before. Where was I going to get four hundred dollars? They were lucky I could find enough money to put gas in the car so I could get to Towaoc and drive them home. And then they passed out on the couch. I don't think I ever really understood what kind of sickness their alcoholism was until that morning. That was the day I finally accepted that neither one of them was ever going to be the parent in our family. I was so mad. I had to get out of there."

Fifteen years and her matter-of-fact retelling of her sad, challenging childhood didn't change how hard it was to hear the things she'd grown up with. The best thing he could do for her then was just to listen.

He was still listening.

"I called Kyle to see if he wanted to hang out or shoot some hoops, and he said he and his big brother had made plans to go hiking, but that I was welcome to join you guys."

"I remember that day. You were, what, seventeen?"

Joanna nodded. "My first thought was 'boring,' but Kyle dared me to go. He said that if I didn't find the day interesting, then he'd buy my lunch for a week. And since I'd just spent my lunch money on gas, it sounded like a decent deal."

"Stinker. He should have bought you lunch, anyway."

She laughed. "I think he took pity on me and did."

"As I recall, you kept challenging me that day. You pointed to everything and said, 'What's this?' 'Where does that path lead?' I believe you were trying to stump me."

"I was," she admitted. "Of course, if you'd given me the wrong answer, I wouldn't have known it. I was so ignorant about nature back then. But even by the end of that first day…" Their pace finally slowed as she allowed herself to reminisce. "I knew you were someone unique, someone special. You had a bond to something so strong that it was almost supernatural to me. You understand the land in a way I never even understood my own family. I wanted to learn your secrets. I wanted to be like you. I wanted a connection like that."

Other than the rhythmic *swish-swish* of their sodden jeans rubbing together with every step, they walked the last few yards to the land bridge in silence. When they reached the rock arch that had been carved out by eons of the Silverton River pouring through its base, Ethan stopped and turned.

He reached for Joanna, even if she didn't need his help to make the step up. "*We* had a connection like that."

She seemed unsure of what to do with the outstretched hand. She was thinking again. Good thoughts? Regrets? But then she slid her palm into his and held on as he pulled her up beside him. "I know. But I destroyed it."

"Sherman Watts destroyed it." Ethan's grip flinched as the old guilt surged through him. "I should have kept you safe."

"I never blamed you. Not once."

"I know that. But you were mine to protect. My responsibility. And I failed you."

"*I* was the failure, Ethan. I didn't know how to fight for what I wanted." She laughed, but it was a sad sound. "I was so messed up, I didn't even know *what* I wanted." She tried to pull her hand away and bow her head, but Ethan wanted to hear this. Hear all of it, finally. No matter how painful it might be, he had to know why she'd left. After tucking his flashlight into his belt, he stroked his fingers across the cool dampness of her cheek and urged her to continue. "All I knew was that I wasn't happy. So, in my eighteen-year-old brain, that meant happiness must be somewhere else. I kind of came up with my own twelve-step plan. Go to college and get a career so I could earn some respect, make some money so I wouldn't be broke every day of my life. Turn myself into somebody who was strong enough to stand up to Sherman and Elmer Watts and others like them. It was too late to do it for myself here on the rez, but I could do it for others. That'd be a bit of payback, and maybe no one else would have to go through what I did."

"So you reinvented yourself as Joanna Rhodes, a smarter, tougher version of the girl I knew. Bound and determined to save her own day."

A wry smile crooked the corner of her lush, pale lips. "I thought I was just surviving. But that does sound like I'm trying to be Superwoman, doesn't it?"

"Sounds like a different story to me. Come on." He urged her ahead of him onto the almost stairlike path of rock worn between the grasses and moss that covered the top of the bridge. With his hand enjoying the delightful assignment of resting on her backside to steady her along the steepest part of the path, he asked, "Did I ever tell you the legend of Sleeping Ute Mountain?"

"I know that if you look at the Ute Mountains from about twenty miles away, their profile looks like a giant Indian lying down on his back. One slope creates his knees, the highest peak forms arms crossed over his chest. There are toes that stick up, a headdress that tapers down to the town of Towaoc."

She'd paid attention in social studies class. With the rain making the mossy stones extra slick, he had her sit to shimmy safely down the opposite side. "You're talking about the shape of the rocks. I'm talking about the ancient story behind them."

He heard her laughing above the spray from the river hitting the rocks below them. "Tell me the story, oh wise one. I'm sure there's a lesson to be learned here."

"The discount version is that in the very old days, the Sleeping Ute Mountain was a Great Warrior God. He came to fight against the Evil Ones in the land. Their battle created the mountains and valleys in the Four Corners area."

"And the blood from the battle created the creeks and rivers?"

"You always were a quick student."

"Fourth in my class at Yale. First in my class with you." She held his hand to pull herself to her feet, then eyed the distance between the rocks and the grassy field beyond and leaped across the muddy bank. "Just how does this legend pertain to me?

Ethan followed her over the mud and continued. "The Great Warrior God defeated the Evil Ones, but he was so wounded that he lay down to rest and fell into a deep sleep. Our ancestors believed that when he is needed, the Great Warrior God will rise again to help them in the fight against their enemies."

"So, the men who murder FBI agents, and rape teenage girls—they're the Evil Ones. And since you're such a part of the land here, you're the Warrior God fighting our modern battle."

"No." He gripped the straps of his pack in front of his chest and looked down at her. She was tall and bedraggled and muddy and gorgeous as she watched him with those dark, expectant eyes. "You are."

Joanna's gaze dropped to the center of his chest. "Nice story." When she looked at him again, he could see she didn't believe. "I don't belong here. I've spent fifteen years making a point of *not* belonging."

"You were born of this place, Joanna. You spent a year with me on this mountain. Yes, you went to Yale, went to Quantico, went to D.C. But you came back when we needed…when your people needed you." He touched the corners of her mouth, nudging it into a smile again. "And the warrior name fits. As I recall, you were the one doing the ass-kicking up at the caves above Cougar Fork."

That earned him a genuine laugh. "That's only because you don't like guns."

"That's because you're fighting for something—the safety of the people on this mission. Justice. Truth. You're a warrior goddess who has returned to help us fight our enemies again."

Her smile didn't need one dot of makeup to turn his head. "Warrior goddess. I like that a lot better than Superwoman."

"It fits." Ethan dipped his head, and when her gaze locked on to his and she didn't pull away, he pressed a kiss to that smile. Joanna's lips were wet and cool with the rain. But after that first tentative contact, they softened and warmed, and parted to welcome him.

He'd have thought a shared conversation, a long walk and a gentle kiss would take him back in time to when he and Joanna first became lovers. But as her fingers curled up beneath his collar and latched on to his neck, as his hands found her hips and pulled her trim curves into the harder lines of his body, as her husky moan matched a similarly needy sound in his throat, Ethan discovered he was firmly rooted in *this* moment. With this particular woman. The old memories were there, yes, but he was making new ones tonight. He tasted the heat inside Joanna's mouth. Their wet clothes sparked a delicious friction and left little to the imagination as she rubbed against him, stretching up on tiptoe to alter and deepen the angle of the kiss.

And Ethan obliged the unspoken request. He was a mature man now, one who'd seen the miracles of life and the worst of death and whose character had been shaped by both. The hunger he felt for this woman went far deeper than the lustful innocence of his youth. His blood surged, his heart opened. He *needed* this connection to be whole again. He found solace in her acceptance, healing in her desire for him. He widened his stance and pulled her into the throbbing response of his body. He cupped the nape of her neck, cradling her head as he plunged his tongue inside her mouth, mimicking all the sweet, sensual things he wanted to do with the rest of her strong, beautiful body.

Ethan wasn't recapturing a sweet moment from the past. He was laying claim to everything he wanted for his future.

If only the woman was willing.

If only she could see a future with him.

A guilty conscience made one hell of a chaperone. He had promises to keep. One, he'd made to Joanna a long time ago—the other, just last night. And neither of them involved throwing her down in a muddy field and making love to her.

"Joanna." He skimmed his lips along her jaw and nuzzled the soft skin beneath her ear. He needed to pull back, to curb the eager wants of his body, to guard his heart before he screwed up the rest of his life by falling in love all over again with a woman determined to leave him. "We need to stop."

"We should." But her lips brushed against his neck, sending a shiver of desire straight down to his groin. His fingers tightened their grip in her hair. "It's been so long since I've wanted…anyone. I'm not afraid when you touch me. I…want…you to touch me."

Ah, sweet mercy. He was fighting to be a good guy here. He nuzzled the wet silk of her hair. She smelled of earth and rain and everything he'd ever wanted.

But he needed to pull it back. They had a job to do. People were counting on them. *She* was counting on him to help her accomplish this crazy-ass mission to bring in Sherman Watts and square off against him in an interview room.

That was what she'd asked of him.

And that was what he'd give her.

"I can't, baby. Not right now. I shouldn't." Reaching down beneath the soles of his boots, Ethan called on a will more powerful than his own to unwind her arms from his neck and pull his lips from the smooth caramel cream of her skin. He cupped her shoulders and put a good six inches of space between them. The rain would cool their clothes and the sensitized skin beneath soon enough. Until the wet and chill and discomfort could steal the moment back, Ethan rested his forehead against hers, savoring the warm breeze of her ragged breaths caressing his cheek, closing his eyes to imprint this precious, tentative connection to Joanna in his mind forever.

"You're right. Bad timing. Job to do." Too sarcastic. Too tough. That was Agent Rhodes talking.

"Listen to me, *Nüa-rü.*" He opened his eyes to absorb the natural beauty of her long dark lashes resting against her cheeks. His own pulse beat like a war drum in his ears, drowning out his brain's attempts to send a message of control to his hormones. "I want to be with you the way the earth wants to see some sunshine tomorrow. But I have to make sure we're in a safe place for the night." A vague notion of the wind shifting or the barometric pressure dropping—of some change in the world outside this cooling embrace crept across his senses.

"And I want to look for Ben a little longer tonight. I—"

Her eyes popped open and looked straight up into his. She heard it, too. "Is that the river?"

"Is that thunder?" they asked in unison.

They separated, turned, searched.

The percussive noise was steady, mechanical—and growing louder by the second.

"Ethan, helicopter!" Joanna pointed to the blinking lights in the northern sky, coming in across the meadow and picking up altitude to clear the bluffs across the river. She waved her arms and shouted. "Hey! Down here!" She turned and gave him a smile. "They must be looking for us. Where's my flashlight?" She ran toward the oncoming bird, fumbling to get her light switched on while she was moving. "Base camp must have gotten at least some of Ben's last radio call and sent it in to pick us up. Get your light. Hurry!"

"Joanna, wait." Ethan jogged after her, feeling less sure about a rescue. Martinez had been adamant about grounding the official helicopter until it was safe enough to fly. "Joanna!"

"Hey! Come back!"

But it whipped past overhead without any indication that the pilot or passengers had seen them.

She was breathing hard from her run by the time he caught up to her. "So much for a rescue. Maybe it was one of those tourist helicopters that flies guests around to show them the scenery. Do they still do that here?"

"Yeah. But not at night. I don't think they were looking for us or the scenery."

Joanna turned, letting him read the thought processes on her face. She'd figured it out, too. "He was flying at night without using a spotlight. He wasn't looking for anything."

Ethan braced his hands on his hips and nodded agreement. "That's something else we'll have to report when we reach base camp. Somebody violated the sheriff's no-fly order. If Watts saw that, too, he'll go even deeper into hiding."

"Unless Watts has a friend with a helicopter who'd give him a ride out of the country?"

"I doubt it."

"Me, too. Although the trace I found at the shooter's position on top of the cave bluff…"

"What?"

"It made me think that Watts wasn't the man shooting at us. That someone else is on the mountain."

"Like who?"

"Maybe that shoe print Miguel Acevedo found *does* belong to Boyd Perkins."

A hit man on the mountain with them? Ethan scanned the limited horizon, automatically sizing up the places where a man could hide—or where a couple could safely escape for the night. That was a dangerous complication this already messed-up search didn't need. They needed to get moving. "Did you see a similar print up top?"

Joanna shook her head. "It was all rock. It's just that what I saw there wasn't what I would have expected from Watts. But then maybe he's trying to throw us off his trail again. Besides, if Boyd Perkins was here, he'd be going after Watts to keep him from talking, not shooting at us, right?"

Ethan wrapped his hand around Joanna's elbow and pulled her into step beside him to get them off the open field and back to the relative safety of the trees and rocks. "I suppose that makes logical sense."

All of a sudden, Joanna planted her feet and twisted her arm from Ethan's grasp. "Wait a minute. The helicopter—you don't think…?"

"What? That Perkins flew in, found where Watts was hiding and killed him?" He started walking again. "I doubt it. Watts thinks like a rat. My guess is he's holed up somewhere nice and tight for the night."

She hurried to catch him. "So what's our next step? Keep looking for Ben?"

"I say we wait and give one last look for him in the morning. The storm will have passed by then, and we'll have the light so we can move quickly and efficiently. Maybe allow ourselves an hour to search. Then we'll need to head on down to base camp to make our report—at least get close enough so we can use a cell phone to call in his disappearance."

"And Watts?"

Ethan stopped, faced her, pinched her chin between his thumb and forefinger. "I said I'd find him for you. It may be delayed a day or so, but I intend to keep that promise. I'll be back out here tomorrow after we handle Ben's disappearance. I'll pick up Watts's trail again."

She closed her fingers around his wrist and pulled it from her chin. But instead of releasing him, she laced her fingers with his, letting him know that she was in this hunt with him for just as long as it took. "So we wait until daylight to resume our search. What are we going to do tonight?"

Ethan tugged on her hand and headed back toward the natural bridge. He already had a plan. "We told HQ we'd be staying on the mountain tonight. I know a dry place where we can warm up and get some sleep."

"Can you find it at night?"

"I could find it blindfolded if I had to."

SHERMAN WATTS STRAINED with the effort it took to keep the sapling bent at an angle while he tied it off. He pushed harder with his legs, tried to make his cold fingers work faster. One. More.

There. He held his breath as he backed away. *Nice work, Sherm. You always were good with your hands.*

"You know it." The voice in his head was female. Familiar. Though strangely out of place. He shook his head to clear the phantoms from his mind, and wound up shaking the ball bearings back and forth inside his skull. "Son of a bitch."

Clutching the brim of his hat, he pulled it down on either side of his head, as though he could keep the raging headache from leaking out of his ears. He plopped down on his backside in the brush and closed his eyes, waiting for the world to stop spinning.

He was in serious need of a drink and racing toward dehydration. He might have laughed at the ironic thought if his stomach wasn't crawling with hunger and he could catch a decent breath.

Where had he gone wrong? What mistake had he made that ended up with him hiking back down toward Marble Mountain and Towaoc? No way could he get back to his borrowed truck and Mesa Ridge or his uncle. The cops would have watches posted around anything remotely connected to him. He couldn't even call his anonymous "friend" at the crime unit and beg a favor. Of course, he shouldn't have needed to. His plan should have worked.

He'd made it all the way up to Rising Sun Creek and had erected a lean-to. He was set to stay up there right until the first snows began to fall again. When he'd heard the blast and rock slide behind him, he knew he'd just cut off any easy access to his remote location. In fact, he'd been feeling so damn fine sure of himself that he'd opened his pack and pulled out his fishing tackle. He'd had to chunk up some of the ice near the bank to get water to drink, but in the deeper pools, he'd be able to find something small and tasty and fresh to grill over a fire.

As far as he was concerned, life didn't get any better than that. The law could just go hang their sorry selves if they thought they were going to mess up *this* gig for him. A man didn't need thousands of dollars and the pressure of answering to any boss, or anyone, period, in order to be happy.

Yeah, he'd toss a line in…

Paradise had ended abruptly when the shooting started.

Sherman dropped his pole, cursed as he watched the current catch it and take it downstream to get jammed in the ice and snapped in two. He'd scrambled back to the lean-to for his pack, had to dig all the way to the bottom of it to find his gun—broke his last new bottle of whiskey in the process.

He'd thrown himself to the ground, crawled on his belly like a snake to the edge of his lookout position. But by the time he'd reached any kind of vantage point, the gunfire had stopped. "What the hell is goin' on?"

Must have been kids from the rez playing with their daddies' guns—kids he'd like to take a stick to for messin' up his… But then the shooting started again. Did the cops think they'd found something? Had they somehow gotten past the caves and picked up his trail again? Did they think they were going to corner him up here like a pack of huntin' dogs surrounding their quarry?

Sherman had lain there in the rain and the muck for a good forty-five minutes before he realized the cops weren't coming. He'd laughed at his success, craved a drink to celebrate it.

He sat up with the sobering thought that if the cops hadn't been shooting at him, then he'd been royally screwed. What were the chances of someone else hiding out on Ute Mountain? Someone armed and dangerous and reckless enough to exchange gunfire with those pesky federal agents?

He hadn't wasted any time pondering about who else might be on the mountain, or what his purpose might be. He wasn't running from just the cops now.

He was running from Boyd Perkins.

Smart money would have bet on him to stick to the high ground because it was so much harder to reach. The chopper he'd heard flying overhead confirmed that as it headed toward the summit of Ute Mountain. That's why he'd chosen this spot down in the gully at the base of Marble Mountain. Perkins wouldn't think to look down here. The trees would warn him if anyone got too close. He could catch some shut-eye now before he made the long trek into Towaoc tomorrow. Once there, he could borrow some wheels and drive down to Mexico.

Then the cops couldn't harass him, Perkins couldn't kill him, and he'd live happily ever after. Maybe he'd change his drink to tequila and live another fifty-eight years just fishing off the end of a boat. Nah. The money here in Kenner County had been good while it lasted, but he didn't need it. It was a good plan.

I don't know anybody more resourceful than you, Sherm. The woman's voice praised him, comforted him. The voice in his head probably should have freaked him out because that sweet, loving woman had abandoned him a long time ago.

But he was tired. He was wet. He was cold.

Lying down, he pulled his pack beneath his head, turning his nose to the tangy scent of sour mash that permeated the damp canvas. With his fingers resting on the gun tucked at the front of his belt, he curled up on the ground with his traps, his headache, his memories of Naomi Kuchu to keep him warm and fell asleep.

Chapter Nine

"I found some more dry fuel in the underbrush. Should be enough to keep the fire going through the night." Ethan announced himself, tossing up an armload of dead tree branches he'd harvested before hoisting himself up and entering the cave again. The last time he'd climbed up without a word, a startled Joanna had whirled around, her Glock poised to blow a hole right in the middle of his chest.

Several apologies and assurances later, he'd gotten a small fire started near the mouth of the raised cave. They'd shared an intimate dinner of energy bars and bottled water by the firelight, and then he'd excused himself to make one more check on the security of their camp farther downstream on the bluff side of the Silverton River.

"The rain's keeping everything quiet," he said, pulling himself in and shoving the wood against the granite wall. "I think we should be able to sleep for a good—"

This time, Ethan was the startled one. He turned around and froze in his tracks.

"I asked you to wait. Didn't you hear?"

How was a healthy man supposed to hear anything when every drop of blood in him was swimming straight south of his belt buckle?

"Ethan?" Joanna stood beside a boulder where she'd laid out her vest and blouse and turtleneck to dry in front of the fire. The wet jeans she'd hurriedly tried to pull on were stuck between her knees and calves and slowly sliding back down toward her feet as she modestly crossed one arm over her breasts and the other over the plain white panties she wore. "You're staring."

"It's still the prettiest view on the whole mountain." She might have blushed, but his gaze hadn't made it up that far yet.

Suddenly, his own soggy clothes felt sticky and hot. She'd spread out their hypothermia blankets on the dirt floor, and though he was sure there was nothing more to it than creating a place to sleep, his body read it as a blatant invitation. And his pulse was tapping out a definite RSVP.

There was a lot to be said for the sexiness of basic underwear, especially when there were so many miles of taut golden skin stretched out in between. The firelight dappled her long, lean curves with a rosy warmth, and he was inspecting every inch of it, from the dimples beside her knees to her hollow little belly button and the nip of her waist to...

"Do you mind turning around?"

"Yeah." He grinned like a schoolboy, ached like a man who'd been too long without the one woman who haunted his dreams.

She muttered something and turned her back to him to battle with the wet denim again. Though, to his way of thinking, this view was just as enticing. "I remember when you used to be a gentleman about things like this."

And he remembered when she'd come flying apart in his arms, all breathless and wide-eyed with wonder, and had asked him when they could do it again.

"I've missed you," he whispered on a ragged breath.

The jeans had made it up to her thighs before she hugged her arms around herself and glanced back over her shoulder. "What am I supposed to say to that?"

"Nothing. I'm turning." Summoning a strength he didn't know he possessed, he managed to turn and study the layers of strata in the wall without really seeing them. "There were so many nights I needed…I needed what we had. I needed you. After that day, did you ever once need…me?"

He breathed in deeply, tried to steady his pulse, tried to look away. But the movement of her hopping on one leg to slide into those uncooperative wet pants drew his attention. The gentle bounce of her breasts, hidden by nothing more than a strip of lace and her long, dark hair, kept it.

"Forget the jeans. We both need to dry off so we can stay warm tonight. Here." He unzipped his vest and draped it over another rock, then went to work on the buttons of his shirt.

"What are you doing?"

"Practical survival. Come on. Lose the pants. I promise to be a gentleman if you promise to avoid hypothermia."

"You're going to strip down to your undies and expect me to think that nothing's going to happen between us tonight?"

He forced himself to turn away and peel off his shirt and the insulated Henley he wore underneath. That was the hell of loving a woman, he supposed. His own body could simmer away unfulfilled, and he wouldn't complain so long as she was taken care of. That was true with this one, especially, who'd already been victimized by men she should have been able to trust.

Ah, hell. A familiar fist punched him in the gut as he imagined just what Sherman Watts and his uncle had said and done to her. Ethan had to say something to lighten his mood, or he'd wind up scaring her further with his own anger. "Well, I prefer to call them boxers or shorts, but I promise, nothing's going to happen tonight unless you ask me."

"But you…" Instead of finishing that argument, she pointed to the unmistakable bulge pushing at the front of his unzipped jeans.

He was sitting on the rock, untying his boots, but he quickly pushed to his feet. "Would you feel more comfortable if I slept outside?"

She seemed to consider it for a moment. But then she shook her head. "You'll freeze."

"Joanna…" He turned away from those big, dark doe eyes and stretched the shirt back over his head. He'd endured worse than arousal on a cold night. "No way in hell do I ever want to say or do anything that reminds you of that bastard."

"Hey." When her fingers brushed the middle of his bare back, he jerked. "Whoa."

With a shared startle like that, he would have expected her to withdraw her touch. But not the Warrior Goddess with the strength to conquer demons. Instead of pulling away, she flattened her hand against his skin, burning him straight down to his bones. But he supposed what he was feeling inside didn't necessarily broadcast through the rest of his body.

"You're chilled already." He looked down over the jut of his shoulder to see the concern stamped on her courageous features. "We're mature enough to handle this. We both need to be strong for tomorrow. And we'll move faster if our clothes have a chance to dry. Confined space, small fire, shared body heat—that's the only way we'll stay warm tonight." She even had the strength to stand there gloriously half-dressed, and smile. "So, you and your boxer shorts are welcome to stay with me."

God, he wanted her. But he wanted—he needed—something else from her even more. He tossed the shirt back over the rock and faced her. "Just to sleep."

"Unless I ask."

"You trust me to do that?"

Those beautiful earth-colored eyes locked on to his for the longest time before she nodded. "I trust you."

Her words were a true gift. One that erased fifteen years of guilt.

By the time Ethan had finished stripping down to his socks and Skivvies, Joanna was sitting on the hypothermia blankets she'd spread on the relatively flat cave floor. "Go ahead and lie down closer to the fire, otherwise I'll block the heat." He untied his knife from his belt and carried it to the far side of their makeshift bed. "Will it bother you if I sleep with this?"

She reached beneath the blankets and pulled out her gun. "Will it bother you if I sleep with this?"

He laughed and lay down beside her, flat on his back with his fingers lightly clasped over his chest. "I'm definitely keeping my hands to myself unless you okay it."

"It's not for you."

He dismissed her apologetic look with a smile and patted the blanket beside him. "I know. Come on over here. Body heat doesn't work unless we're closer."

At first she lay down on her left side, facing the fire. Ethan matched her position, scooting up behind her and pulling the top blanket over them. He had his left arm curled beneath his head for a pillow, but his right arm couldn't seem to find a comfortable—impersonal— place to settle. Stretching it out along the length of his body put a hitch in his shoulder. He tried resting it on Joanna's hip, but even as he recognized a possessive sense of rightness by claiming the curve, she squirmed. So he moved it a little higher to let it curve over her waist. But she twisted again, hunching her shoulders and moving away from him.

"Joanna." He pulled his arm away and rolled onto his back with a sigh. With a granite mattress beneath them, it was no surprise to feel her still wriggling to find a comfy position. But he suspected this was something more. "Are you sure you don't want me to sleep outside? I take up a lot of room. Maybe more than you might be comfortable with."

"No. It's just…" She rolled onto her back and turned her face to his. "I don't want you behind me. I thought it wouldn't matter, but…I haven't actually *slept* with a man since…" She squeezed her eyes shut, working past a tough moment, before opening them again and boldly meeting his gaze. "That's how Watts—"

Ah, hell. Ethan didn't need to hear the rest of that ex- planation. He shifted onto his side and pulled Joanna into his arms, lying with her face-to-face, settling her cheek on the pillow of his shoulder. Their legs tangled together and he hugged her tight. She didn't have to say another word as she curled her arms between them and settled against him with a sigh.

He brushed her hair off her face and let it fall down her back. "Better?"

She closed her eyes and he felt the tension leave her body. "Much."

Much better. He smiled over her head, watching the light from the fire dance across the walls of the cave. His body was a little worse for wear, his bed was hard, but Ethan felt as though he was settling in for the best sleep of his life. He pressed a kiss to Joanna's temple. "Good night, *Nüa-rü.*"

"Good night, Ethan."

An hour or so later, the storm had eased into a light patter of rain and Ethan was dozing in a pool of languid heat. He had Joanna in his arms. They were hidden and safe. He'd just added some more wood to the fire to at least keep the embers glowing until dawn.

But something wasn't right. There was a low, almost moaning sound filtering into his dreams. Then he became aware of something lightly tapping against his chest and he roused himself to take clear stock of his surroundings.

The touches became the unintended caress of Joanna's fingers bumping against him as she twisted and worked her fingers in that nervous habit of hers. The moan became a whisper of words. "Just say it. He'll never hurt you. You can do this."

"Hey."

Joanna fell silent as soon as she realized he was awake.

"Who are you talking to?" He wrapped one hand around both of hers, stilling their fretting movements. She held herself so still, so stiffly, that Ethan grew immediately concerned. He brushed her hair off her face to read the clarity of her eyes. "You weren't having a nightmare, were you?"

She shook her head. "I was psyching myself up."

"For what?"

"You don't have any protection, do you?"

Ethan reached for his knife and sat up, instantly on alert. "Did you hear something?"

"No." She pushed his hand and his knife back to the ground, sitting up beside him. "Not that kind of protection."

If this was a dream, Ethan had no intention of waking up.

"I want you. I want to try."

JOANNA FELT AS THOUGH it were her first time all over again when Ethan returned to the blankets and pulled her on top of him. "I think you should know that I…" With one forearm propped atop his chest, she traced the column of his neck and the strong line of his shoulder with her finger. It was a shy, girlish thing to do, but she didn't want to spook him or herself by moving things along as quickly as her feverish body seemed to want. "I'm not any more experienced at this kind of stuff than I was before the rape."

His dark eyes reflected the firelight and seemed to glow from within. The tiny muscle that pulsed along his jaw revealed anger on her behalf that she'd been forced that way, but those beautiful onyx eyes showed her nothing but patience and desire.. "Anything you want, *Nüa-rü*. Anything you don't want. You tell me. I want this to be right for you."

He was all heat and muscle, coppery-skinned and supple right down to the waistband of his black shorts. He was such a big, broad specimen of masculinity that even with her tall, athletic frame, Joanna felt feminine and delicate, by comparison. "Can we just start slow and see where it goes? Is that asking too much?"

When she drew her finger across the tension in his jaw, he turned and caught the tip of her finger with his lips and gave it a delicate suckle that seemed pull a taut response from deep inside her. "Anything," he reminded her.

And for now, that *anything* meant taking their time reacquainting themselves with each other's body. Moving in no more of a hurry than the gentle rain falling outside, they touched with their hands and toes, their lips and bodies.

As Joanna tasted the smooth line of his jaw, she curled her toes against the rougher texture of his leg. Ethan settled his palm over the curve of her bottom, warming her skin through the thin layer of cotton between them. If she wasn't kissing his mouth, then his lips were busy exploring her eyelids, her cheek, the newly discovered bundle of nerves beneath her right ear.

She nuzzled his skin at the juncture where his neck and shoulder met and breathed in the invigorating smells of rain and the outdoors. She touched her lips to the point of his chin, gently nipping at the salty tang of his skin there. He lifted the weight of her hair and drew lazy circles that tickled the skin of her nape, making her muscles bunch and quiver, again and again, creating a growing friction between their stomachs and chests with each helpless shimmy.

Her legs parted and caught his thick, muscular thigh in between. When he bent his knee, pressing against the warmest, neediest part of her, a knot of molten heat ignited at her core.

Joanna buried her face against his neck and moaned at the pressure building inside her. Her skin was extra sensitive to every touch, her lips extra needy to every kiss. The warmth inside grew fluid and flowed through her blood like a river rising, growing with speed and power. Every sensation felt new, unfamiliar, as if her body had forgotten what it felt like to be sexual. To want. To catch fire and need a thing the way she needed Ethan.

"You keep making sweet sounds like that, babe, and I don't know how much longer I can handle slow and easy." His voice vibrated against her skin like a drowsy caress.

"Touch me, Ethan. So I can really feel it. Touch me."

He stroked his big hands—callused and firm enough to arouse, gentle enough to soothe and reassure—up and down her back. Each pass of his hands was slightly different. He reached between them to skim his thumbs over the tips of her breasts, to flick, to tease. He reached a little lower the next time to slip inside her panties to squeeze her bottom, to move her hips over the heavy evidence of his arousal.

"More," she begged, catching his bottom lip between her teeth and giving him a gentle nip.

He laughed deep in his throat and gave her lip the same little nip.

"More."

"You're sure?"

"I'm sure."

The next pass of his hands unhooked her bra. In another move, the bra was gone and he was lifting her, dragging her up to claim her breast with his mouth. He swirled his tongue around the hard button at the tip, then pulled on it. Gently, harder. Gentle again. Then more demanding, until Joanna was writhing on top of him, wanting more, wanting everything.

"Ethan…" she gasped. "Ethan."

He sat up, spilling her onto his lap, dipping his head to catch the other, neglected breast in his mouth and torment her with his tongue. She raked her fingers across his scalp and held him against her. "Tell me what you want, babe."

"I want you. Now," she demanded.

He raised his head and smiled against her mouth before he claimed it in a deep, drugging kiss. In a matter of seconds, her panties were gone, his shorts were off and she was back in his lap with his sheathed, throbbing desire nudging against her.

He brushed her hair off her face and smoothed its length down the line of her back. In a moment of calm before the certain storm, he rested his forehead against hers, looking deep into her eyes, deep inside her. "This is what you want?"

Would he really stop now? Yes. If she asked it of him. Because he was Ethan—her teacher, her lover, her protector and friend. He was the earth that gave an anchor to her wind.

"I want this," she assured him, winding her arms around his neck and lifting herself against the wall of his chest, feeling herself primed and ready to become a sexual woman again. "As long as I can see your face. I want to know it's you."

He pulled her legs out on either side of him, his hands guiding her into position in his lap. He'd decided not to crush her with his weight. Whether it was consideration for the hardness of the floor or the trauma of her past, it was a beautiful thing to do. With two fingers he pointed to his eyes. "You look right here, *Nüa-rü*. Right here."

She held her breath as he entered her. She didn't blink or look away as her body adjusted to the size and feel of him inside her.

"You okay?" he asked. She could see it in his face, in the stretch of muscles across his chest, what it was costing him to be so patient with her.

She nodded, smiled, loved him for it. "I think I'm going to be better than okay. I can do this. With you, I can do this."

And then, with a kiss, with his arms wrapped tightly around her, he began to move inside her. He showed her what it was to want a man, to trust a man, to be with a man again.

Had she ever felt this alive? This whole? This desired? Her entire world was this man, this moment. There was no past. There was no tomorrow. There were no fears. No doubts. No fifteen years apart. There was just her. And Ethan.

She tipped her head back, her cries of joy echoing inside the cave as he brought her to the peak of pleasure and they tumbled down the other side, together.

ETHAN WOKE AGAIN, some time later, with a naked woman sprawled like the best kind of blanket across his chest. The relative silence of the cave told him the rain had finally stopped and the fire was dying. He felt warm, rejuvenated, content. His arms and heart were full, his world in perfect alignment. With Joanna in his arms, he was at peace.

"I'd forgotten how hard you sleep…right after. Don't worry. I kept an eye on things while you were out."

"*You* were watching over *me?*"

"Warrior Goddess and all that, remember?"

He smiled at the voice that didn't know whether to be shy or seductive. Joanna had always managed to be an intriguing mixture of both. He opened his eyes to find her serene smile just in reach of his lips, and he lifted his head to gently claim them. "You okay?"

"I'm better than I thought I'd be. No regrets."

Words of healing to a once-broken heart. "Me, either."

When he rested his head back on the blanket, she settled in on top of him. "I think one of us wound up with the more comfortable bed last night. How are you doing?"

He propped one hand beneath his head and with the other, played with the midnight silk of her hair, smoothing the tangles, crumbling a tiny clump of dried mud and brushing it away. "I've had worse nights, believe me."

"So. When can we do it again?"

Ethan laughed. "I guess some things never change, do they?" Catching her around her waist, he rolled them onto their sides facing each other. Her long hair tumbled over her face and he loved catching it and combing his fingers through it all the way to the ends as he pulled it back and took in his fill of her classic Native American features and long, lithe body.

But then, some things did change. His eyes and fingers were drawn to the small white scar that marked the golden tan at the top of her left breast. "Is this what he did to you?"

She batted away his hand and quickly covered the spot with her own. "Does that turn you off?"

"No. Hell no." He dipped his head and kissed the mark. Then he caught her mouth and gave her a hard kiss, telling her in no uncertain terms just how beautiful she was to him. "It's a badge of honor. Of all you've been through. Of how you survived. But when I'm reminded of how much you were hurt, I just…" His fingers clenched convulsively at her waist.

"You want to hurt *him?*" Were his coarser, unenlightened instincts that obvious? She pried his hand from her waist and laced her fingers together with his. "Get in line. My therapist said those kinds of feelings are healthy and normal. Unless you get obsessive about it, of course. It's okay to feel anger. To feel rage. Some days you don't, as time goes on. More days than not. And sometimes it hits you so hard you want to scream or punch something. That's normal, too."

"But I'm not the one who was hurt."

"You were collateral damage, Ethan. And I'm sorry for the part I played in that."

"Leaving me wasn't your fault."

"It wasn't my fault I got raped, either. It still hurts, though, doesn't it?" No argument there. Her dark eyes showed an understanding he was just now beginning to accept. "It changes how you deal with people, how you live your life."

And there the understanding stopped. The connection he and Joanna had resurrected during their time here on the mountain was destined to end.

Joanna dealt with life by committing herself to a career because it was safer than committing herself to a relationship. He'd made love to Joanna Kuchu last night. But FBI agent Joanna Rhodes was leaving come Monday, or as soon as they found Watts and her interview was finished.

Then he and Joanna would be finished.

Again.

The predawn chill filled the cave. Their fire must have died.

Ethan pressed one last kiss to her lips and sat up, bracing his elbows against his knees, steeling himself for the day ahead. Trying desperately to steel his heart against loving her, as well. "Looks like the sun will be up soon. We'd better get dressed."

She sat up beside him, pulling the crinkly blanket up over her breasts and laying a gentle hand on his arm. "Do we need to talk about this?"

No. Talking wouldn't make the inevitable any easier to take. Ethan pushed to his feet and walked buck naked over to the fire pit to stir the embers and add the last of the fuel. "I'll get us some fresh water we can heat up. I've got a couple of coffee packs in my bag."

Joanna squinched up her face, accepting the abrupt change in topic, if not necessarily approving the avoidance tactic. "Not that nasty stuff you used to bring on camping trips? Why don't you just boil some tree bark?"

"Hey. It survives anything and it's hot." He pulled on

his shorts and jeans and checked the dryness of his boots. "You want to crimp your taste buds, try eating MREs for a month."

"That's right. Elizabeth said you served a stint in the army. That you went to Afghanistan. That explains the haircut."

He let the boots sit for a few minutes longer and picked up his shirts. "Six years as an army ranger. I specialized in casualty recovery."

"Casualty…?" The crinkle of stiff material told him Joanna had risen. She wrapped the material around her as she began to dress. "You brought back the dead?"

"Or wounded. Or lost."

"Search and rescue. Why doesn't that surprise me? You've done that your whole life, haven't you—finding souls and saving them?"

"No." He thought of that night in his truck when Joanna had left him. He thought of Sam Keller putting a gun to his head in the middle of a battlefield because he'd seen too much blood and death. Saving souls? Ethan hadn't saved the ones who counted the most. "Sometimes, I lose them."

She wasn't a fool to miss the hidden meaning in that remark. But he was done with this conversation.

"Gear up. If we don't find any trace of Ben in an hour, we're heading back down to base camp."

Chapter Ten

"Nothing." Ethan sounded frustrated, grim.

Joanna came up beside him as he pushed to his feet. "But you're sure the helicopter landed here?"

Though the storm and wind had beaten down much of the strawlike grass and wildflowers just beginning to bud out on the high meadow across the Silverton River, even Joanna could now see that something heavy had crushed the vegetation here. An exploration along the lee side of the river in the sunlight had turned up nothing new on Agent Parrish's disappearance—no shred of clothing, no shoe prints, no body. But after their allotted hour of futile searching, Ethan and Joanna had reluctantly started their trek back to the command post where they hoped that by some miracle, Ben and the rest of the KCCU had somehow found each other.

It was a miracle that Ethan, with his keen eye and that sixth sense that was tied to the land, had noticed the differences in the flattened plants at the far edge of the meadow. But the discovery of anything useful stopped there.

A helicopter landed." He tossed aside a stalk of

scrub grass he'd been inspecting. "If there was any trace of blood left behind, it's been washed away. There's no way of knowing if Ben made it this far and got picked up by a rescue team or a good Samaritan, or even if the chopper we saw is the same one that set down here."

He walked to the edge of the grass, where wind and water erosion had worn away the soil and root system that held it in place, shearing it down to bare rock. Ethan jumped down to the gravelly incline below the cut and reached up for Joanna's hand. He held on firmly, giving her the balance she needed to make the same five-foot jump and land gracefully on her feet.

But just as soon as she nodded her thanks, he released her and headed for the first hairpin turn that would take them back and forth at a modest rate of descent into the forested gully about thirteen hundred feet below. The plan was to find Elk Thunder Creek at the bottom and follow it on out to the trail head where the KCCU had set up their temporary camp.

So that was how it was going to be this morning, hmm? Back to the taciturn Indian who refused to say a lot because he didn't want to waste words. And he said that *she* was two people.

She missed the Ethan she'd walked with and talked with last night. He'd reminded her of a time when she'd been open to new experiences, hopeful that there was something better for her out there in the world—if she could learn enough, and be tenacious enough to go after it.

She missed the Ethan who'd been so patient with her last night. The man who'd kissed her so thoroughly, had loved her so well. In the quiet seclusion of that cave, they'd formed a bond that felt deeper, richer, mor precious than the love they'd shared before the rape. Last night, Ethan had listened to her fears, adjusted to her needs—he'd made her feel like a whole, normal woman again instead of the unemotional shell who normally walked through every day of her life.

But somewhere between giving him her trust and the dawn of a new day, their fragile new bond had been buried inside that cave, altered the way yesterday's rock slide had changed the shape of Ute Mountain. For them, there could only be the present. The reality of their missing partner's uncertain future, and the omnipresent shadow of her tragic past, demanded their attention this morning.

He wanted to protect her. She needed to be independent.

He talked about lost souls and relentless demons, of letting them go before they consumed her. She wanted to hunt hers down and look him in the eye.

He was a man of the earth. She was the restless wind.

He belonged in Kenner County. Her career was in Washington, D.C.

How could they ever make the magic of their time on the mountain the reality of their everyday lives?

Today, there were no easy conversations, not even arguments, no lessons to be taught. There was just walking and silence—and an uncertain wish that somehow her world and his could meet and meld and survive for more than one night.

ELK THUNDER CREEK was much narrower and more shallow than the Silverton River. But with snowmelt and the heavy rains feeding it, the water tumbling below eet was just as noisy.

use." She shut off her cell phone to save the

battery, and tucked it back into her pack. She raised her voice to tear Ethan's focus from the small pines that blanketed the short, steep drop to the creek. "We're still too far out to get reception."

He nodded, indicating he'd heard. "We'll try again after another mile."

When he didn't face her, or give any indication of climbing back up to the path where she stood, Joanna grabbed on to one small tree after another to join him at the creek bed. "What is it? Do you see something?"

Though relationship discussions were apparently taboo this morning, he hadn't hesitated to share information about a danger in their path or any possible clue that might lead them to Ben Parrish or Sherman Watts. He hunched down to bring his shoulders level with hers, and pointed to a stand of young trees across the creek. "Look at those pine saplings. The trunks have all been broken near the roots."

"Could it be from flooding?" she suggested, eyeing the line where mud met drier soil just beyond her feet. "Looks like the water level is already going down. If this was moving even half as fast as the Silverton, it'd mow down pretty much anything that size or smaller."

"I don't think that's it. Look." With one long stride, he stepped across the creek and pointed to the watermark about halfway up one trunk. "Here's where the creek crested. They were standing tall when that happened."

Joanna needed to take a short run at it, but she, too, crossed the creek to investigate more closely. She touched one of the thigh-high boulders at the edge of the water. "It looks as though something made a nes here. With the rocks to provide a windbreak, bending the trees over creates a small shelter."

Ethan was down on one knee, sifting through a spongy bed of wet leaves and pine needles. "*Things* that build nests don't use wires to hold them together." He pulled a strand of copper wire from the stacked-up leaves.

Bracing her hand on his knee, Joanna knelt beside him and began to imagine the size and shape of a grown man curled up beneath the canopy of saplings. A surge of adrenaline kicked up the beat of her pulse. "Do you think Ben spent the night here?" She was already scanning the slopes on both sides of the creek, looking for footprints in or out of the deep V of the landscape besides their own. "Why wouldn't he come back to us if he survived that fall and the river? Could a disoriented man make it this far?"

"Easy, Sherlock." Ethan caught her chin between the gentle pinch of his fingers and directed her gaze to the evidence at hand. The skin cells beneath his touch instantly leaped to attention. *She* came to attention when his hand settled over hers at his knee, as if he was reaching out to her one more time, holding on to something he knew he was about to lose.

What did he know that she didn't? "What is it?"

His expression hardened.

"You have to look at all the information." He twirled the wire in front of her eyes. She looked closer. Finally recognized it. Understood.

Sherman Watts.

Her awareness of Ethan's shifting mood turned into ̶ ̶ ̶ferent kind of awareness. "Watts was here ̶ ̶"

He nodded, made no effort to reclaim her hand as she stood and surveyed more carefully each way in or out of the gully. He zipped the wire into a vest pocket and pushed to his feet. "This matches the filament we found at the blast site. Something is making Watts head back toward civilization instead of sticking to the high country."

"The helicopter?"

"Who knows? But he's moving south, southwest— on about the same course we are. And…"

"And?"

An internal debate darkened Ethan's eyes and lined his expression. Her breathing quickened, deepened with anticipation before he finally made his decision to speak. "The leaves at the bottom of that shelter still hold a little warmth. He's not that far ahead of us."

Ethan's reluctance to share that bit of news was probably in direct proportion to her eagerness to act on it.

They had one more chance to catch Sherman Watts. She had one more chance to bring in her rapist and face him across an interview table—today. Now. She had one more chance to break him in every legal way possible. The key to solving Julie Grainger's murder could be lurking in this very stretch of woodland.

"We have to go after him." Joanna circled the rocks, looking for one of those hidden signs that Ethan rarely missed. "Can you tell what side of the creek he's on now? Is he on the path? Cutting through the trees?"

"Give me a minute."

She came back to him, tugged at his sleeve. "I understand the need to get word to the others about Ben. But if something happened to him, and Watts gets away…Ben's sacrifice will have been for nothing." She pleaded with him to understand. "Sherman Watts can't get away from us again, Ethan. I need to face him."

"Don't worry, you'll get the chance to do your job. I promised I'd find him for you, and I will. But the bastard's armed and more than a little bit desperate if he had to change his escape route. We need to be cautious."

Joanna pulled away as soon as he touched her, tried to protect her from the challenge that was hers to face. "I need to do this before I get it in my head that I can't."

"He'll be drunk or detoxing, either of which makes his behavior unpredictable. The man already blew up half a mountainside trying to throw us off his trail—I don't think we can be too careful about dealing with him." He checked his watch and scanned the horizon. "We could make it to base camp in another two hours, an hour and a half if we book it. We'll return with backup, surround him."

She didn't have two hours, not even an hour and a half before she'd lose the mental advantage they had right now over Watts.

Joanna knelt down and picked up a stick to poke it through the bottom of the man-made nest, looking for a clue that would point an arrow toward the man they were after. Maybe some of the wet leaves would stick to his boots and leave a trail. She dropped the stick and began to search the surrounding ground, looking for remnants of leaves that matched the bedding in size and shape and color. These were too light a green. Those too long and narrow. "How long do you think he's been gone?" She looked up when he didn't immediately answer. "Ethan, how long?"

He knew. She could see it in the hard glint of his onyx

eyes. That damn mystical sixth sense of his knew which way Sherman Watts had gone. He knew where to find him. "Probably a matter of minutes."

She rolled back on her heels and stood. She wrapped her hand around a small tree to help pull herself up the steep incline. "Then we can catch him. Don't tell me to wait for backup when we're this close. I've already waited fifteen years."

"Joanna—"

"Look." A muddy boot print. A dark green leaf like the ones in the shelter. She followed them up the hill. "Tracks. Right here. Right through here." Topping the gully, she found another print, embedded with the same leaves, and a flatter path. "They go up right beside that broken sapling. Come on."

"Joanna—wait!"

She was vaguely aware of Ethan charging up the slope behind her. She turned, stepped.

Snap.

She felt the telltale give of tension beneath her foot. The milliseconds of each reaction passed by like watching a movie one still frame at a time.

Not a broken tree.

Ethan shouting her name.

Copper trip wire beneath her foot.

A sleek brown missile hurtling toward her.

With another blink, real time returned and she couldn't move fast enough. Joanna jumped, braced for the certain impact of the pine tree whipping toward her. But in a blur of motion, Ethan slammed his arms around her and spun, taking the brunt of the collision.

Like a spring-loaded catapult, the tree hit hard

enough to lift them off their feet and launch them into the gully. *Oof.* "Hell."

They hit the ground hard and rolled, toppling end over end until the cold splash of water at the bottom stopped them.

Joanna lay on her stomach for a moment—stunned, dizzy, feeling damn lucky she hadn't broken her neck. The creek water streamed over her dangling hand, its biting chill rousing her as effectively as a dose of smelling salts. She pulled her hand from the water and rose onto her bruised knees. "Ethan?"

She'd been snug in his arms. Safe, as always. But now she was alone. Where was he? That sapling must have hit him like the front grill of a speeding car. She staggered to her feet. Turned. "Ethan!"

Wading ankle-deep into the creek, Joanna grabbed his big, still form as he floated into the current, and tugged him to the bank. With a groan of effort, she dug in her heels and fisted her hands in his clothes, dragging him several feet up the slope before laying him down and falling to her knees beside him.

How badly was he hurt?

Why wasn't he moving?

Why the hell was she crying now, when she needed to see what she was doing?

"Ethan?" She checked his pulse and thankfully found a strong one beating beneath the cold skin of his neck. After a quick, loving caress to the sculpt of his cheek, she checked his head, his neck. Cuts. Scrapes. Bumps. Nothing as serious as she'd expected. "Come on, big guy. I need you to talk to me. I need you."

She unzipped his vest and laid her ear to his chest,

listening to make sure he was breathing. All at once, his lungs expanded with a deep, agonizing groan and he tried to sit up. "Ah, hell."

"Ethan!" Joanna eased him back to the ground. She pressed a quick kiss to his lips and squeezed his hand, studying his hooded eyes all the while to make sure their focus was clear. "Don't move. Relax. For a minute there, I thought I'd lost you."

The hand she held down at his side tightened around hers with the subtly reassuring grip she recognized. "Now you know how I felt when you left me," he whispered, letting his eyes close again.

"So this is some cosmic lesson you're trying to teach me? I don't like it. Nobody's dying on me today. Get it?"

A tight smile flickered between the white lines of pain bracketing his mouth. "I'm sorry, baby. I'm not dying." He breathed in, groaned. "It just hurts like the blazes."

She smoothed her hand across his cheek again, brushing away the chilly moisture from the creek. "Did you hit your head? Where does it hurt?"

"Just had the wind knocked out of me."

"I'm sorry. This is the second time you've saved my life. I should have looked more carefully, but I was so anxious to get Watts. I didn't mean for you to get hurt. Ever."

"Shh." He raised his hand to brush the tears off her cheek. "Don't you cry for me, *Nüa-rü.* I'm a tough old army ranger. I've survived worse." Though that taut muscle in his jaw pulsed, his breathing seemed to be evening out. "Are you injured?"

"Nothing to worry about. Just lie still."

"I always worry."

"I know." Finally moving far enough past the fear to

think like an FBI agent and not a woman who'd nearly lost her man, Joanna swiped away any lingering tears and shrugged out of her backpack to find a first aid kit. "Does it feel like anything's broken?"

"I'll be fine."

A blot of crimson seeping through his clothes at the left side of his waist drew her attention. "Don't tell me you're fine. You're bleeding."

As she unzipped his gear vest and pulled it open, Ethan leaned onto an elbow and tried to push himself upright. "Watts could still be in the area. Forget me and—"

"I am not forgetting you. I could never forget you. Now lie still until I check every inch of you." She stepped over his legs and knelt to check the wound. "You must have a pretty deep laceration. Wait. I said to lie down."

Ethan groaned a mighty curse as he fought off her attempt to ease him back to the ground. "If he rigged up one tree, then there'll be other traps out here. Who knows what other sick tricks he's prepared for us? We can't stay here in the open."

"Fine." She peeled aside his vest. "Then let me get you wrapped up enough so you can move." When she caught sight of raw flesh, Joanna's own muscles clenched at the pain he must be feeling. "Oh, my God."

The sapling Sherman Watts had tied to the ground had whipped Ethan as effectively as a cat-o'-nine-tails. The force of the blow had cut right through his clothing and left bleeding red welts along his left flank.

"I need to borrow this." With her hand at his belt, she untied his hunting knife and pulled it from its leather sheath. She unpacked gauze and sterile salve from the first-aid kit and set to work slicing his shirts and vest open and cleaning the wounds.

Any disorientation he'd felt earlier had cleared. His grip was firm as he pulled her hands from their work, and his mood was turning grumpier by the minute. "I said we can't stay here. Watts is close. I sense it. I know it."

"We're not going anywhere until I'm sure you can be moved. If one of those ribs is broken, it could puncture a lung." She twisted her hand free and gently probed his side. A wince and a curse were enough to confirm her suspicions. "They could just be bruised or cracked, but I'm definitely wrapping these."

"Fine. But not here." He bent his knees, trying to get his legs under him. "Help me up. Take me back to camp. You're right. I need medical attention. We can't stay here."

"Damn it, Ethan. I wear a badge and gun. I can take care of myself. I've been taking care of myself my whole life. I can damn well take care of you, too."

The discussion ended abruptly at the tiniest of sounds from the woods above them.

A single step.

Moments later, a handful of pebbles cascaded down the steep slope and rolled beneath the surface of the water.

Joanna's hands stilled over the gauze she'd taped to Ethan's wounds. He'd heard it, too.

Everything inside her tensed. Waited. Listened.

"No." He tried to grab her wrist, but she moved more quickly than the stiffness of his injuries allowed. She crawled a few feet up the slope, pinpointing the direction of the sound. "Joanna," Ethan growled through gritted teeth.

"Stay put."

Stretching out onto her belly to keep her profile as low as possible, Joanna pulled her gun and shimmied up to the top of the slope to see what kind of company they had.

But she already knew.

Creeping through the underbrush like the cockroach he was, she saw him. Thin black hair, hanging in long oily tendrils across his shoulders. Dark, squinty eyes.

Sherman Watts.

"Don't you—" This time, Ethan couldn't stop her. He rolled onto his hands and knees, tried to stand. "Joanna, no! Not on your own!"

The hunt on Ute Mountain had all come down to this. She sprang from her position and gave chase.

Her blood simmered, speeding the pace of her heart. Her chest expanded, giving her the oxygen she needed to race across the flats. Her vision was razor sharp, taking in roots, dips, rocks and other obstacles in her path while she closed the distance between them. A hundred yards. Sixty. Forty.

Had he actually come out of hiding to see what kind of damage he'd done to them? To gloat? To finish the job? Had he seen the long black hair and realized just who it was pursuing him?

You can do this, girl. Look who has the power now, you SOB.

He scurried away from the creek, over the next slope and down the other side, his wide-brimmed black hat quickly disappearing beyond her line of sight.

Joanna slowed her pace and quieted her footsteps, listening to the sounds of a pudgy fifty-eight-year-old knocking his way through the trees and brushes. Sliding.

Falling. Cursing. She used that moment to top the hill without being seen.

And plummeted down the same washout that Watts had stumbled upon. Joanna slid a good twenty feet through the mud and gravel on her bottom before her feet hit solid ground and stuck. Ah, but fifteen years of intense physical training versus a lifetime of drinking too much and avoiding honest work paid off in spades. She was closing in before Watts could even get on his feet again.

"Sherman Watts! I'm a federal agent. Stop where you are!" She paused long enough to point her gun into the sky and fire off a warning shot. Birds screeched and cawed and took flight from the trees. Her lungs burned, but she dug down a little deeper and shouted a fair warning. "Come peacefully and it will go easier for you!"

His response was to turn with his gun drawn and fire wide of her position.

Joanna dove for cover. "Don't make me shoot you!"

She didn't want him dead. She wanted him to answer for all he had done.

But he was zigzagging away through the trees, huffing back up the incline. Joanna breathed in deeply, in through her nose, out through her mouth. She pushed herself to her feet and ran after him.

Twenty yards. Ten.

Close enough to hear the ragged rales of his breathing. Close enough to see the sweat staining the back of his denim jacket. "Drop your weapon and get on the ground!"

"Get away from me, bitch!" he rasped, and turned, raised his gun.

Joanna never broke stride, never hesitated. She barreled into his gut full force and knocked him flat on his ass.

His gun went flying. They rolled over her bruised wrist and she yelped at the pain, losing her grip on her own weapon.

Armed, unarmed—didn't matter. She was a different woman than the last time they'd exchanged violent blows. She wasn't going to lose this fight.

When his fist came at her, she locked her arm and deflected the blow. She rammed her fist against his throat. He slapped wildly at her, gurgled with the pain she caused him. When he spotted a gun and lunged for it, she caught his knees with her feet and knocked him to the ground, quickly stretching, diving to retrieve the weapon herself.

But one thing about the disgusting cockroaches of the world—they had an innate knack for survival.

As Joanna's fingertips touched the grip of her Glock, she heard the ominous ratchet and click of a bullet sliding into the firing chamber of a gun. Joanna froze.

"Get your hand…away…from that gun, you bitch." As halting and gaspy as the threat was, she believed it.

For one awful moment, her stomach heaved, her body clenched with an instinctive fear. But in the next breath, she found an inner calm—from her FBI training or her lessons with Ethan, she didn't know. He'd once held a knife to her throat. Today it was a gun to the back of her head. She wasn't going to be his victim anymore.

"Put the gun down," she suggested calmly. "Threatening a federal agent is not a good idea."

"I don't care what you think. I ain't goin' nowhere with anybody. I'm disappearing into the world. Understand? I've got nothing to say to you."

"Well, I've got a thing or two to say to you."

Rolling onto her back despite his huff of protest, Joanna looked up into the blotchy red face of her rapist. Other than a few more pounds and a nose that was purple and swollen from years of alcohol abuse, her squinty-eyed nightmare looked pretty much the same as she remembered. "I'm arresting you on suspicion of—"

"Naomi?" His face spasmed with shock. The gun wavered.

Joanna pushed up onto her elbows. "I'm Agent Joanna Rhodes of the FBI."

"Shut up! You're dead." He raised the gun, steadied it enough to aim at her chest. "Or you will be."

Watts's body jerked and Joanna's entire body jolted in response. Her fingers dug into the mud beside her as she instinctively clutched her chest.

"Get away from her, you son of a bitch."

The threat, as fierce and low and wonderful as any sound she'd ever heard, flowed through her like the spirit of the mountain rising from the ground itself. There was no bullet hole, no pain. She hadn't been shot.

Watts, on the other hand, began to tremble. His fingers popped open and his gun fell to the ground. Joanna wisely scrambled after it and picked it up before he collapsed to his knees. He turned to the voice behind him and she saw a long, wicked-edged hunting knife protruding from the back of his shoulder.

"You stabbed me," he whined, dropping to his knees.

Joanna looked up at the warriorlike intensity of Ethan's eyes. He stood tall, erect—but tattered and pale—clutching his left arm to his side, with blood already seeping through the bandages she'd wrapped around his ribs.

How could she not love him?

"Does it hurt?" Ethan's nostrils flared with every deep, painful breath.

"Hell yes."

"Good." Ethan pulled the knife from Watts's shoulder, ignoring his yelp of pain. He wiped the blade on his pant leg and wandered off a few feet, where he lowered himself to the ground and endured his own pain in noble silence. "Don't worry. You're not going to die from that wound. It's not any worse than what you did to me."

Watts tried to reach the wound over his shoulder, and cursed at the blood that stained his fingertips. "What the hell kind of cop are you?"

"He's not a cop." Joanna was on her feet. "But I am." She picked up his gun and stuck it in the waist of her filthy, muddy jeans. She holstered her own weapon and pulled out the handcuffs attached to her belt. Kicking his feet apart to put him flat on the ground, Joanna knelt beside Watts and pulled his wrists behind his back, ignoring his plea to spare him pain. "Sherman Watts, you're under arrest for assaulting a federal officer—maybe two or three of us—grand theft auto, resisting arrest, accessory to murder—"

"What?"

"And whatever else I can think of once I catch my breath." She quickly read him his rights. "Do you understand?"

"Yeah."

"Good. Now lie there and shut up until I'm ready to talk to you."

"And you?" She went to Ethan, gently checked for further injuries, then clasped her palm around the back of his neck and kissed him very, very thoroughly. By the time she pulled away, he'd returned the favor. His hand lingered at the back of her neck, massaging her nape as she ripped off the placket of his flannel shirt and used it to secure one of the gauze bandages over his ribs back into place. "You're really wreaking havoc on my quest for independence, you know that? That's the third time you've saved my life."

"I said I wasn't going to let you face that bastard alone." He gingerly inhaled a deep breath and leaned in to rest his forehead against hers. "Get used to it."

THE KCCU BASE CAMP was a hive of activity. Calls were being made. Machinery was being dismantled and packed away. Sherman Watts was handcuffed in one ambulance, getting stitched up by a paramedic and treated for dehydration. While two other medics tended to his injuries, Ethan sat at the back of a different ambulance, debriefing Sheriff Martinez, Tom Ryan and Dylan Acevedo on the status of their friend and fellow agent, Ben Parrish.

An extra helicopter was being called in. Search teams were being formed. Dr. Callie MacBride-Ryan and Miguel Acevedo from the crime lab had their heads bent over the shell casings and copper wire Joanna and Ethan had brought back from the crime scenes on the mountain.

Joanna sat in the middle of the chaos, wrapped in a blanket and sipping a cup of hot, bitter coffee. Up on the mountain, she and Ethan had worked—and loved— like partners who understood and complemented each other the way the earth and the wind, the fire and water created a balance of all that was needed to survive. But here, she was an element out of sync with the world around her.

Yes, she'd given her preliminary report to Martinez. She'd personally thanked Bart Flemming for rigging up whatever kind of super cell he had that finally enabled her to call for a chopper to evac her, her patient and her prisoner safely and quickly down to the command center. And she'd already given herself three separate pep talks to keep her calm and focused and ready to interrogate Watts as soon as the medics cleared him and he was transported back to the station house.

Her gaze slid over to Ethan across the parking lot. Even in the middle of a tense, animated conversation, he sensed her and looked over Agent Acevedo's head to meet her gaze. *I love you,* she whispered on a thought. If there was any way she could find a place in his world where she was so out of sync, if he could break his ties with the land and become a part of hers...

His dark eyes narrowed, questioned, as the medics lifted his gurney into the back of the ambulance. Joanna blinked and looked away, hating the pitiful signals she must sending. The man was going to the hospital for X-rays and a deep debriefing of his wounds. He didn't need to worry about her when he should be taking care of himself.

"Agent Rhodes?"

Joanna pulled herself from her thoughts and turned to meet Elizabeth Reddawn's polite smile. The older woman had brought her the coffee earlier. Now she was opening a plastic container of wrapped sandwiches. "I imagine you haven't had much solid food the past couple of days and it's almost dinnertime. These are from the Morning Ray Café. Personally, I like the pimento cheese on sourdough. But you can't go wrong with a turkey and swiss on rye, either."

Though she had no appetite, Joanna knew she'd need every bit of her strength to face Watts. She picked the first sandwich sitting on top. "Thank you."

"Ham and cheese kind of girl, eh? Enjoy." Elizabeth snapped the lid back into place and moved on, heading for the communications table where Bart was, once again, underneath the table connecting or disconnecting some cord.

Connect. Disconnect.

A lightbulb went off inside her head. It couldn't really be that easy, could it? Just plug herself in somewhere? Make herself a place where she belonged? When had she ever *not* had to fight for anything she wanted in this world?

Joanna threw off her blanket and hurried after the sandwich lady. "Elizabeth?" The petite Indian woman stopped and turned, smiling expectantly as she approached. *You can do this, Joanna. You can do it.* "I know I wasn't as friendly as I should have been when I first arrived, and I wanted to apologize for my rudeness."

Elizabeth tutted, waving aside the apology. "You weren't rude, honey."

"I was."

"I expect certain memories make it hard for you to be here."

Joanna nodded. She wasn't used to doing this, but over the past two days, she'd proven to herself that she was strong enough to do anything. "I need to ask you a favor."

"Sure."

"I have to go to the sheriff's office to write my report and—" she thumbed over her shoulder toward the ambulance where Watts was being treated "—and take care of some business. Would you ride with Ethan to the hospital? Make sure he lets the doctors take a look at him and, and…"

Elizabeth took her hand and winked as she leaned in to whisper. "And call you to let you know how he's doing? Of course I will. I care about Ethan, too."

"Thank you." Elizabeth smiled and turned to finish her deliveries and get her things, but on impulse, Joanna kept hold of her hand and pulled her attention back to her. Elizabeth turned with a question on her face.

Joanna squeezed the older woman's hand and declared herself a friend. "And you call me Joanna."

That earned her an even bigger smile. Elizabeth patted her hand and promised, "I'll call you as soon as I know anything. Joanna."

Joanna nodded, feeling something warm and hopeful—and maybe just as strong as her rigid independence.

She'd made her first connection.

Chapter Eleven

Joanna rose from her chair, adjusting the hem of her suit jacket and buttoning it as she strolled around the interview room's gray metal table.

"Being drunk isn't a defense." Her voice was articulate, clear, unemotional save for the scoffing note of pity she had in reply for Sherman Watts's last statement regarding his motive for his crimes. "They don't serve whiskey in prison, you know."

"That's a shame. I'd have gone long ago."

The creep thought she'd find his lowlife sense of humor amusing? She'd already gotten him to sign a statement about his activities on Ute Mountain. Threatening her with a gun, planting explosives, rigging the tree that had cracked three of Ethan's ribs and earned him twenty stitches. Though he adamantly claimed he'd never shot at any human being in his life, she had him dead to rights on enough charges to keep him in prison for a very long time.

Yes, he'd stolen a truck. Yes, he'd *borrowed* the explosives he'd found in the back of it. Yes, he'd set several traps on the mountain, including a couple he proudly announced she and Ethan hadn't been smart enough to find—she'd already alerted the forensic team that Ethan's friend Garan Coons was leading up the mountain tomorrow to be on the lookout for the hidden dangers.

But he claimed to have done all that because he was guarding the exact whereabouts of his favorite fishing hole and had wanted to ensure himself a little privacy.

The one thing she hadn't gotten him to talk about was Boyd Perkins, and his association with the hit man and Julie Grainger's murder.

Logic hadn't worked. Nice talk certainly hadn't.

But the man's fingers were drumming almost uncontrollably against the side of the table where he was handcuffed. He was detoxing, probably feeling a nasty headache and some stomach gripes. The knife wound on his shoulder hadn't injured anything vital, and would probably leave an attractive scar to make him look a little tougher to his comrades behind bars. But without allowing him anything more than a couple of aspirins to dull the pain, he was probably aching pretty good right about now. His efforts to remain cavalier and play stupid to those questions were beginning to cost him.

Time to push him a little further over that nervous edge.

She knew she had an audience taking down every word on the other side of that two-way mirror and on the camera recording Bart Flemming was making in the observation room. But this show she was gearing up for was for Sherman Watts alone. *Do it, Joanna. No matter what he says, no matter how he reacts, get in his face and do it.*

You are stronger than this bastard ever imagined.

Joanna turned, coming in right beside him, brushing

her arm against his as she braced her hands on the table. "Here's what's going to happen to you, Sherm. You're going down for Agent Grainger's murder. With DNA from that leather necklace of yours, we can put you at the site where her body was found. That's not a life sentence, that's a death penalty."

"I didn't kill no FBI agent."

"Yeah?" She leaned in, getting right in his face. "She was a woman, wasn't she? Women are nothing to you. They're trash you use up and throw away, just like those bottles you suck dry every day of your life. If she got in your way, if she didn't do what you wanted, you'd take care of her. You'd put her in her place. You like beating up on women, don't you, Sherm?"

"That woman wasn't beaten!"

Joanna straightened. Walked around to her side of the table and softened her voice to a more reasonable timbre. "Now, how do you know that?"

His head shot up. His dark eyes glared. He dropped his gaze when she didn't so much as blink. "Okay. I was there. I helped throw her body into the river, but she was already dead, I swear."

"Who hired you to dispose of the body? Who's been paying you ten thousand dollars a month for the past six months?" She smacked the tabletop, startling him when he didn't immediately answer. "Who hired you?"

Bam. She'd hit the trigger.

His chair toppled backward and crashed to the floor as he rose to face off against her. "Look, bitch—I don't owe you anything. There are scarier people in the world to be afraid of than you, with your mouth and your gun and your hair—thinking you're all that.

Thinking you can use me to get what you want. That ain't right!"

Joanna dodged to the side as he shoved the heavy metal table at her, and sent it screeching into the wall behind her. She put her hand in the air, waving off the cadre of agents and deputies no doubt running to that door to rescue her right now. She kept her eyes on Watts's sad, sour, superior expression as he dragged the table behind him, advancing on her. "You think you've got something on me. You think you're smarter. I can handle you."

When he lunged at her, she twisted his arm behind him and put him down, face-first, on the table. "Yeah. You did that real well. Who *can't* you handle, Sherm? Who are you afraid of if you're not afraid of me?"

Trapped in the ignominious position, shaking as the rage and whiskey and fear worked through his system, Sherman Watts suddenly seemed like a scraggly, pathetic little man—not the nightmare who had turned her teenage world upside down.

She had the advantage. She didn't even have to talk tough anymore. "Now we're going to walk back here and have a seat. You and I are going to have a nice little chat." Once he'd pulled the table back into place and righted his chair, Joanna sat back down across from him. She asked the fifty-million-dollar question. "Did Boyd Perkins kill Agent Grainger? Is he the man who hired you to help cover up the crime? To help him hide out on the reservation so he could continue looking for a crime family's missing money?"

"He'll kill me if he knows I talked to you. I think he tried to kill me already when I was up on Ute Mountain. Can you give me some kind of protection?"

"I'll see what I can do."

At last, he nodded. "Then I want a lawyer. I'll tell you what I know."

"All right. Let me get someone to take your statement." Feeling less victorious over an enemy than she felt the satisfaction of knowing she'd done her job well, Joanna got up and headed for the door.

"Agent Rhodes?"

She turned.

"I know something else. If I tell you, you'll make that death penalty thing go away, right?"

"It depends on what you tell me."

"I don't have a name but…Perkins and me, well… he's got a man on the inside. Somebody who works with you. He's got our numbers and he…well, he called me and told me you all were lookin' for me. I know he calls Boyd Perkins, too."

Sheriff Martinez's suspected leak. So there was a traitor in their midst. Joanna slid her gaze to the window, knowing each of them was hearing this, too. But Watts was more interested in how the information was going to affect him.

"So, even without a name, you're gonna take murder one off the table, aren't you?"

"That's for the courts to decide. But if you're lucky, you'll get out of prison for one last drink before you die of old age."

"What kind of crack is that?" For one fleeting moment, his eyes narrowed, and she thought she detected a glimmer of recognition—not that she was Naomi Kuchu's daughter, but something else, something much, much more personal. But if any recollection of the day he'd violently used her body to repay an emotional and monetary debt had passed through his mind, he must have dismissed it as some kind of drunken hallucination. "You speak to me with respect, girl. This is a legal situation. You don't want me suing you for harassment. You owe me that much."

Joanna would never be able to simply dismiss the crime, but now she could move past it. She could heal. She could put Sherman Watts behind her. Forever.

She opened the door. "Mr. Watts, I don't *owe* you a damn thing."

WHEN JOANNA CLOSED that interview room door behind her and walked into the beginning of a brand-new life, the first thing she walked into was the solid wall of Ethan Bia's chest.

Literally. She instantly pulled back from his deep-pitched groan, taking in the green hospital shirt and the thick ridges of bandages wrapping his chest underneath. His skin color was good, coppery and warm, his eyes glinted like finely polished onyx.

And while Joanna stood there in an openmouthed stupor in the KCCU hallway, he wedged a finger beneath her chin to close her mouth before leaning down to press the lightest of kisses to her lips.

"You okay?" he asked.

"Ethan." She clutched her fingers into fists, then uncurled them. She wanted to touch him. But she might hurt him, and what was he doing here, anyway? "You're supposed to be in the hospital. Elizabeth told me they were keeping you overnight."

He caught her fingers in one big hand and stilled

their nervous flexing. "Were you not just in that room alone with Sherman Watts?"

"You know I was."

"Did I not promise that I would never let you face that man alone again?"

"You did."

"Don't you trust me to keep my word to you?"

One heartbeat passed. And then another. And then Joanna was stretching up on her toes and winding her arms around his neck. "I do."

She supposed this PDA wasn't the most professional behavior Martinez could list in his recommendation letter to her supervisor in D.C. She was marginally aware of people passing back and forth in the hallway, discreetly looking away or covering up a laugh as Ethan held her lightly against his chest and she willingly, eagerly—not wanting to aggravate his injuries, of course—kissed him back.

It was when the hallway had quieted and she was simply leaning close, her head tucked beneath Ethan's chin, that a different conversation did catch her attention. The tones were hushed, urgent and probably meant to be private.

"I can't shake it, Miguel," a young woman said, trying to hide the fear in her voice. "It was definitely Boyd Perkins I saw in my vision. I sense his presence close by, creeping around in the shadows where we can't see him—and he's looking for something. Do you believe me?"

Miguel Acevedo's voice she recognized. Though the tender tone was a new twist from his usual sarcastic humor. "Well, after what I just heard from Sherman

Watts, I'm not going to say I disbelieve. Come on, I think we ought to talk to Sheriff Martinez about it."

"I know you're a skeptic, but I felt this one particularly strongly. Thank you for listening."

"I'll always listen, sweetheart. Always." When they rounded the corner, Joanna pulled away, concerned by the distress she'd heard in the woman's voice. Miguel had his arm around the brunette's shoulders, pressing a kiss to her temple, when he realized they had company in the hallway. The woman with him seemed a little shy, but judging by the way she clung to Miguel's waist, it was very clear that they were a couple. "Hey, big guy," Miguel greeted them. "You're looking a little worse for wear, there. Ethan, you remember my wife, Emma."

"Of course." He smiled as he kissed Emma's cheek. "I heard you two eloped to Vegas. Congratulations."

"Thanks." He turned to his new wife and completed the introductions. "Emma, this is Agent Joanna Rhodes. She's the newest member of our team. She played Watts like a Steinway in the interview room."

The *team* appellation felt good. It felt like she might have earned a little respect, and maybe a friend or two more here in Kenner County.

"Pleased to meet you, Agent Rhodes." Emma Acevedo smiled warmly and extended her hand.

"It's Joanna Kuchu, actually." Yeah. It felt right, shaking Emma's hand and saying those words. "Kuchu is my Ute name. It means 'buffalo.'"

It meant a lot more to Ethan.

At least, once he pulled her into the empty interview room and stopped kissing her long enough, he seemed impressed that she had used her given name.

Joanna stood between his legs as he sat on the table, looking at her with those mysterious eyes and lightly brushing that wayward strand of hair off her face. "Has Joanna Kuchu really come home?"

She reached up to stroke her finger over the proud contours of his cheek and jaw. "I want to stay. I've been doing a little research."

She felt the muscle bunch along his jaw, heard him breathe in deeply to force himself to relax. "When did you have time for that?"

"On the ride into town from Sleeping Ute Mountain. Bart let me use his laptop."

"Sounds like you work too much." His second deep breath echoed her own. "So tell me about this research. What does it have to do with staying in Kenner City?"

All right. She'd thought this through. She knew the details. She had a plan. "I found out there's no trained profiler or interrogation specialist in the Durango FBI office. I could be the first one in the area—consult with the crime unit here in Kenner City and serve the entire Four Corners area. Maybe one day I could select and train my own team."

"Sounds ambitious. But then you always did dream big." His hand settled at the nape of her neck, the skin-to-skin contact warming her straight down to her toes. "I'd like to point out that Durango is a hell of a lot closer to Kenner City and the reservation than Washington, D.C. But it's a lot smaller, too. You might see a lot less action in this part of the country."

Joanna smiled—nothing fake, nothing forced. It was a genuine, unburdened smile. "I don't care about that. Seems like I've seen plenty of action here these past few days." She tiptoed her fingers around his neck and tried to look as deep into his soul as he'd found his way into hers. "I never considered dreaming dreams about this place. I always thought a better life for me was out there somewhere. The only dream I ever had about the reservation was making a life with you."

"Joanna," he growled on a dark husk of emotion.

She pressed her fingers to his lips to silence him. "No. Let me say this. That was the dream I had before everything changed—the rape, Sheriff Watts, feeling so suffocated by the shame and rage and helplessness I felt in this place. Now I understand the healing powers of coming home. That is the most important lesson you've ever taught me, Ethan."

He moved his hands down to her hips and pulled her close enough to rest his forehead against hers. "Tell me more about that dream about a life with me."

"I want to make things work for us if it's not too late." She looked straight up into his beautiful eyes. "I love you, Ethan. Maybe I forgot how to for a little while. But I feel it inside me, burning stronger than ever. I know what that kind of love means now—how much I need to treasure it." She took a deep breath and then laid her heart in his hands. "I know I have some issues...but maybe if we work on them together... Do you think you could have that kind of patience with me?"

The perpetual spring rain might have started falling once again outside. But when Ethan smiled down at her, she felt sunshine. She felt hope.

"Hell, woman. I waited fifteen years for you. I think I know how to be patient."

He palmed her bottom and pulled her up against his

chest, holding her tight, kissing her and kissing her and kissing her, groaning with a mix of pain and delight. When they finally found the courage to ease some space between them, knowing that the connection between them would never be broken again, Joanna smiled against his mouth. "All right. I just spilled my guts. It's your turn to say something now."

Ever a man to choose his words carefully, Ethan had only three for her now. "I love you."

Joanna was finally where she was supposed to be. With Ethan.

Epilogue

"Over here!" Ethan shouted over the rumble of thunder and unceasing drumbeat of rain. "I found a shoe print. Too big to be the kid's, though."

He dropped his flashlight beside him and gritted his teeth against the aching stiffness in his rib cage so that he could pull off his KCCU jacket and lay it over the vanishing evidence.

The Griffin Vaughn estate was a huge expanse of house and land and hidden tunnels underneath, where crime boss Vincent Del Gardo had once lived and died. And now someone had used those same tunnels to get inside the millionaire's high-tech mansion and kidnap his three-year-old son, Luke.

Ethan hadn't even gotten Joanna back to her hotel room or asked her out on a proper date when the call had come in. All available agents, deputies, CSIs and support staff had been called in to search the grounds for any trace of the boy and what might have happened to him. While Sheriff Martinez interviewed Vaughn and his new wife, Sophie, a forensic team was dusting the interior for any prints or other trace evidence. Meanwhile, Ethan was leading a team over the grounds before this damn storm washed away anything helpful out here.

"Miguel!" he shouted again. He'd found a print outside one of the tunnel entrances that reminded him of the fancy-soled hiking boot they'd found at Sherman Watts's trailer just three nights ago. But the rain and runoff from the tunnel's domed entrance was quickly washing it away. He needed to get up, make his voice heard over the storm. "Miguel! You coming?"

Before Ethan could push to his feet, Joanna was there, grabbing his flashlight and bracing herself against his uninjured side to help him stand. Miguel ran up seconds later. He lifted Ethan's jacket and shook his head. "Would've, should've, could've. That print is too far gone to make a comparison."

Lightning flashed in the sky, illuminating the worry on their faces. Joanna voiced what they were all feeling. "How's a three-year-old boy ever going to survive a night like this?"

After a crackle of static, an announcement came over all three of their radios at the same time. It was Callie MacBride-Ryan, one of the forensic specialists working inside the house. "It's a match. The fingerprint I found on the basement stair rail belongs to Boyd Perkins. He took the boy. I repeat. It's Boyd Perkins. He's back in town. He took the boy."

Miguel swore. "I hate it when Emma's visions are right. The damn thing is, they're always right. I'd better get in the house to see if I can help out."

Once Ethan and Joanna were alone again, she shook off the water from his jacket and draped it over his shoulders. "Now will you let me take you to the hospital?"

"It doesn't fit Perkins's profile to want to hurt the boy. Odds are, he's using him for leverage—to get money, or information. Still…" He didn't need to feel her fingers tucking and smoothing his wet clothes into place to know how worried she was—about him, about little Luke Vaughn—about changing her plans for the future to include him, to include *them*.

Ethan tucked his finger beneath her chin and let her see the conviction he felt. "He's Kenner County stock, *Nüa-rü*. That means he's strong. You survived when you had to. The boy will survive, too."

Ethan felt Joanna's fingers lacing with his down at his side. They squeezed each other's hands, sharing their strength, sharing their unique connection to the Four Corners area and to each other.

Together, Ethan and Joanna, Martinez, the crime lab, Agents Ryan and Acevedo and all their support staff formed a formidable team.

The bad guys didn't stand a chance.

* * * * *

Kenner County Crime Unit continues with
SHE'S POSITIVE, coming next month,
from reader favorite Delores Fossen
and only in Harlequin Intrigue!

*Celebrate 60 years of pure reading pleasure
with Harlequin®!*

*Harlequin Presents® is proud to introduce its
gripping new miniseries,*
THE ROYAL HOUSE OF KAREDES.
*An exquisite coronation diamond, split as a symbol of
a warring royal family's feud, is missing! But
whoever reunites the diamond halves will rule all....*

*Welcome to eight brand-new titles that unfold to
reveal the stories of kings and queens, princes and
princesses torn apart by pride and power, but finally
reunited by love.*

Step into the world of Karedes with
BILLIONAIRE PRINCE, PREGNANT MISTRESS
Available July 2009 from Harlequin Presents®.

ALEXANDROS KAREDES, SNOW DUSTING the shoulders of his leather jacket and glittering like jewels in his dark hair, stood at the door. Maria felt the blood drain from her head.

"Good evening, Ms. Santos."

His voice was as she remembered it. Deep. Husky. Perfect English, but with the faintest hint of a Greek accent. And cold, as cold as it had been that awful morning she would never forget, when he'd accused her of horrible things, called her terrible names....

"Aren't you going to ask me in?"

She fought for composure. Last time they'd faced each other, they'd been on his turf. Now they were on hers. She was in command here, and that meant everything.

"There's a sign on the door downstairs," she said, her tone every bit as frigid as his. "It says, 'No soliciting or vagrants.'"

His lips drew back in a wolfish grin. "Very amusing."

"What do you want, Prince Alexandros?"

A tight smile eased across his mouth and it killed her that even now, knowing he was a vicious, arrogant man, she couldn't help but notice what a handsome mouth it was. Chiseled. Generous. Beautiful, like the rest of him, which made him living proof that beauty could, indeed, be only skin deep.

"Such formality, Maria. You were hardly so proper the last time we were together."

She knew his choice of words was deliberate. She felt her face heat; she couldn't help that but she damned well didn't have to let him lure her into a verbal sparring match.

"I'll ask you once more, your highness. What do you want?"

"Ask me in and I'll tell you."

"I have no intention of asking you in. Tell me why you're here or don't. It's your choice, just as it will be my choice to shut the door in your face."

He laughed. It infuriated her but she could hardly blame him. He was tall—six-two, six-three—and though he stood with one shoulder leaning against the door frame, hands tucked casually into the pockets of the jacket, his pose was deceptive. He was strong, with the leanly muscled body of a well-trained athlete.

She remembered his body with painful clarity. The feel of him under her hands. The power of him moving over her. The taste of him on her tongue.

Suddenly, he straightened, his laughter gone. "I have not come this distance to stand in your doorway," he said coldly, "and I am not going to leave until I am ready to do so. I suggest you stand aside and stop behaving like a petulant child."

A petulant child? Was that what he thought? This man who had spent hours making love to her and had then accused her of—of trading her body for profit?

Except it had not been love, it had been sex. And the sooner she got rid of him, the better.

She let go of the doorknob and stepped aside. "You have five minutes."

He strolled past her, bringing cold air and the scent of the night with him. She swung toward him, arms folded. He reached past her, pushed the door closed, then folded his arms, too. She wanted to open the door again but she'd be damned if she was going to get into a who's-in-charge-here argument with him. She was in charge, and he would surely see a tussle over the ground rules as a sign of weakness.

Instead, she looked past him at the big clock above her work table.

"Ten seconds gone," she said briskly. "You're wasting time, your highness."

"What I have to say will take longer than five minutes."

"Then you'll just have to learn to economize. More than five minutes, I'll call the police."

Instantly, his hand was wrapped around her wrist. He tugged her toward him, his dark-chocolate eyes almost black with anger.

"You do that and I'll tell every tabloid shark I can contact about how Maria Santos tried to buy a five-hundred-thousand-dollar commission by seducing a prince." He smiled thinly. "They'll lap it up."

* * * * *

*What will it take for this billionaire prince to realize
he's falling in love with his mistress…?
Look for*
BILLIONAIRE PRINCE, PREGNANT MISTRESS
*by Sandra Marton
Available July 2009
from Harlequin Presents®.*

We'll be spotlighting a different series every month throughout 2009 to celebrate our 60th anniversary.

Look for Harlequin® Presents in July!

TWO CROWNS, TWO ISLANDS, ONE LEGACY

A royal family, torn apart by pride and its lust for power, reunited by purity and passion

Step into the world of Karedes beginning this July with

BILLIONAIRE PRINCE, PREGNANT MISTRESS
by
Sandra Marton

Eight volumes to collect and treasure!

In 2009 Harlequin celebrates
60 years of pure reading pleasure!

We're marking this occasion by offering
16 **FREE** full books to download and read.

Visit

www.HarlequinCelebrates.com

to choose from a variety of
great romance stories
that are absolutely **FREE!**

(Total approximate retail value of $60)

We invite you to visit and share the Web site
with your friends, family
and anyone who enjoys reading.

From *New York Times*
bestselling authors

CARLA NEGGERS

SUSAN MALLERY
KAREN HARPER

More Than Words:
STORIES OF STRENGTH

They're your neighbors, your aunts, your sisters and your best friends. They're women across North America committed to changing and enriching lives, one good deed at a time. Three of these exceptional women have been selected as recipients of Harlequin's More Than Words award. And three *New York Times* bestselling authors have kindly offered their creativity to write original short stories inspired by these real-life heroines.

Visit **www.HarlequinMoreThanWords.com**
to find out more, or to nominate
a real-life heroine in your life.

Proceeds from the sale of this book will be reinvested in Harlequin's charitable initiatives.

Available in March 2009 wherever books are sold.

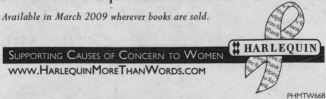

INTRODUCING THE FIFTH ANNUAL
MORE THAN WORDS ANTHOLOGY

Five bestselling authors
Five real-life heroines

A little comfort, caring and compassion go a long way toward making the world a better place. Just ask the dedicated women handpicked from countless worthy nominees across North America to become this year's recipients of Harlequin's More Than Words award. To celebrate their accomplishments, five bestselling authors have honored the winners by writing short stories inspired by these real-life heroines.

New stories inspired by real women who've changed lives

HEATHER GRAHAM

New York Times bestselling author

More Than Words
VOLUME 5

CANDACE CAMP
STEPHANIE BOND
BRENDA JACKSON
TARA TAYLOR QUINN

Visit **www.HarlequinMoreThanWords.com**
to find out more, or to nominate
a real-life heroine in your life.

Proceeds from the sale of this book will be reinvested in Harlequin's charitable initiatives.

Available in April 2009 wherever books are sold.

REQUEST YOUR FREE BOOKS!

2 FREE NOVELS PLUS 2 FREE GIFTS!

◆ HARLEQUIN®

INTRIGUE®

Breathtaking Romantic Suspense

H109R

**Stay up-to-date
on all your romance
reading news!**

The Inside Romance
newsletter is a **FREE**
quarterly newsletter
highlighting
our upcoming
series releases
and promotions!

**Go to
eHarlequin.com/InsideRomance**
**or e-mail us at
InsideRomance@Harlequin.com
to sign up to receive
your FREE newsletter today!**

You can also subscribe by writing to us at: HARLEQUIN BOOKS
Attention: Customer Service Department
P.O. Box 9057, Buffalo, NY 14269-9057

Please allow 4-6 weeks for delivery of the first issue by mail.

IRNBPA0109

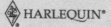 **HARLEQUIN®**

INTRIGUE°

COMING NEXT MONTH

Available July 14, 2009

#1143 SHOWDOWN IN WEST TEXAS by Amanda Stevens
Her photo is in the hands of a hit man, but she has no idea. Lucky for her, an ex-cop stumbled upon the would-be killer...and he's determined to protect the woman whose face he can't forget.

#1144 SHE'S POSITIVE by Dolores Fossen
Kenner County Crime Unit
After discovering she's pregnant, the hotshot FBI agent's soon-to-be ex-wife falls into the hands of a dangerous criminal. He'll do anything to save her life and their second chance at love.

#1145 SMALL-TOWN SECRETS by Debra Webb
Colby Agency: Elite Reconnaissance Division
Only a top investigator at the Colby Agency can help her confront the dark secrets of her childhood—and give her the love and protection she needs for the future they desire together.

#1146 PREGNESIA by Carla Cassidy
The Recovery Men
While working at Recovery Inc., a former navy SEAL repossesses a car...which just happens to have an unconscious pregnant woman in the backseat. Unwilling to let her and her unborn child come to harm, he's ready to shield her for the long-term.

#1147 MOUNTAIN INVESTIGATION by Jessica Andersen
Bear Claw Creek Crime Lab
She was just a means to an end—use her to find the murderers of his colleagues. But the sexy target rouses more than just the FBI agent's need for revenge as they brave the wilds of Colorado in search of an elusive killer....

#1148 CAPTIVE OF THE DESERT KING by Donna Young
A king finds himself attracted to an assertive American reporter, but past hurts have made him suspicious of women. When rebels shoot down their plane, they are in a race across the desert for their lives... and love.

www.eHarlequin.com

HICNMBPA0609